D1563386

Appalachian Patterns

Appalachian Patterns

Stories by Bo Ball

Readers & Writers Short Stories Showcase
Edited by Stanley Beitler

INDEPENDENCE PUBLISHERS INC.
Atlanta, Georgia

Published by
Independence Publishers Inc.
P.O. Box 29905
Atlanta, Georgia 30359

First Printing
Library of Congress Catalog Card Number: 88-080882
ISBN 0-9457440-00-X
Independence Publishers Inc.
Pittsburgh, PA

ACKNOWLEDGEMENT These stories have appeared previously in the following publications, some in slightly different form: "What's in the Woods for Pretty Bird?," Reprinted from *Prairie Schooner* by permission of University of Nebraska Press, Copyright © 1977, University of Nebraska Press; "Heart Leaves," *Crescent Review;* "The Quilt," *Southern Humanities Review;* "The Garden," (Appalachian Patterns II), *Carolina Quarterly;* "The Changing of the Guard," *The Roanoke Review;* "Myrtie's Salvation," *South Carolina Review;* "Idie Red, Idie Blue," *Western Humanities Review.* "Wish Book" and "Heart Leaves" also appeared previously in *The Pushcart Prize V* and *X* editions.

For Those in the Marbled Pattern of Our Kinship Quilt:
Eleanor, Ross, Eb, Pat, Cotton, Hattie, Edith.

CONTENTS

For Daisy Mae—
May all your
patterns be gentle, kind.
Bo Ball

What's in the Woods for Pretty Bird?

WHAT'S IN THE WOODS FOR PRETTY BIRD?

She tried to catch a glimpse of herself in his shaving mirror, but his head and hands, applying Wildroot, crowded what dawn the little washstand glass could hold.

She put his streak-of-lean and eggs on a plate and centered it before the only chair at the table. The biscuits — catheads, he called them — she gave a platter to themselves, beside the bowl of cream gravy. She poured his coffee into the big brown cup that told him to go to Ruby Falls in Tennessee.

She lifted an eye from the stove to help the oil lamp light his breakfast.

"Any sweetenin'?" he asked.

She fetched the molasses from the cupboard. She let him turn the lid, for she liked to see the flesh play on his hands when he bunched it up for a purpose.

She packed his dinner bucket with brown-sugar biscuits and more streak-of-lean. Then she crossed her arms and waited by the stove. She lowered her eyes to watch some wood ants and a granddaddy-long-legs travel the worn roses of the linoleum.

"I dreamt I took me a long trip last night," he said. He split two biscuits into fours for molasses and gravy.

"Tell it me," she said. She hoped it was home to West Virginia, backwards to things she knew, when he rode a milk-white horse to Shady Springs and sang to her. Spark plugs, chokes, mufflers, mud flaps, they sounded like boogeymen in ghost tales she hadn't heard.

"My Willis an' me went all the way to Washington, D.C., right up to the White House door."

"Is 'at back home?" she asked.

"Not hardly. Out a East Virginia to the tip a Maryland."

His dream was crossing state lines before she could help his chewing slow it down.

"Who was with ye?"

"Just me an' my jeep. Takin' curves to get somewheres."

She never had a dream of her own. When she thought she was dreaming, her fingertips traveled to her eyes to find the lashes batting. She liked to be in his dreams, but here lately he filled them with strangers. On Saturdays, he left her on the mountain and took his dreams to town. Spread them for more strangers.

"Till we got to Saltville. Then I picked me up a little flame-headed woman. Hitchhikin' with a red thumbnail." His fork sawed a streak-of-lean in two. "She had some apple brandy in a little red purse with diamonds on the velvet an' we sipped." His throat sounded coffee. "We rested round Roanoke."

He always spared her the ground or grass their bodies found for resting.

"Toward dawn, I stopped to take me a stretch an' give the radiator cap a rest"—he raised his arms, fork in hand, to show how tall he could be sitting down—"an' my billfold didn't climb up my butt. I dropped my hand down. The bulge was gone. Greenback, driver's license, social security, 1-A card, all my identification."

She knew what the redhead would get next. One night, in their first of three houses, she pilfered his pocketbook to find see did he have their marriage license. He didn't. She found instead pictures of him alone, in a cowboy hat or bareheaded, with painted women pasted to his cheek. She lit a match to burn the women. He woke and ran naked to try to catch her in the woods. She slept that night on a cold mossy bank and thought of Barbary Allen.

"I got back calm in my saddle an' asked her could I have another sip a apple. When she unstrung the mouth a 'at red purse, I grabbed it." He poured new molasses on the capped head of another biscuit. "She fought for the pouch, but I downed what brandy was left an' hid my wallet between my legs." His knees cracked together through starched denim. "She bristled into a bobcat, scratched for my eyes. Plucked on my ribs." He was ticklish of his ribs. "I missed a big truck by a hair."

His voice dropped. He was staring straight ahead into the mirror above the washstand, making his black moustaches dance sideways. When he was asleep and the moon lighted him, she liked to watch the moustaches breathe.

"I grabbed her by her crimson curls an' wound 'em 'round her neck."

Last week he had smothered a raven-haired under a featherbed. Some he chopped to pieces.

"I throwed the corpse into the river 'at flows through East Virginia. Then me an' the President we had us a long talk."

"The Holy Ghost is roamin' the woods out there." He didn't hear her. He rose from the table and pulled out his pocketwatch to see where the hands were walking. Then he went to the mirror to check see did the eggs stain him.

He righted a wave beyond the part. He jangled through change to find keys. He cocked his boots for his jeep. "Expect me when you see my face." He didn't turn around. "Got some trees to put my mark on." His job was printing X's on sound timber for the saws.

She blew out the lamp to save kerosene. She ate in his plate. When she heard the jeep echo around the third curve, she buttoned his little radio on and through static for "The Wildwood Flower." She couldn't find it. She settled for "Wayfarin' Stranger." She turned it down low to spare the batteries for his news of wars in foreign lands. He didn't know she slipped to listen.

Her gravy was cold, but she didn't mind.

When fiddles started sawing out something she didn't know, she buttoned them off and rose to rinse the plate. It gave her her reflection: the same yellow curls her head had held for sixteen years, but the brown eyes looked strange. She smiled to try to drain the wildness out. She let the other dishes soak.

She went to the second room to gather his dirty clothes from the bed posts. "Wash on Monday. Iron on Tuesday," she remembered from her two years of education before her mama disappeared and left her with the old deaf woman who held her home from school. She inspected his work pants. He wore a clean pair every day. No green stains from resting on foreign grass with painted women, but in one of yesterday's pockets she felt her daily prize. Her fingers trembled as they inched it out. She read the first half—"Baby"—in red letters. She knew she'd follow. And there she was—"Ruth"—in lettering just as bold. "Ruth when as a Baby," she whispered. She blushed.

She also knew how to read the names of Dick, Jane, Spot, Frog, from her schooling, and Jewel, from him that had it. He taught her his name in their second home in East Kentucky, so she wouldn't open his letters.

She let the crinkly paper brush her cheek. Smelled the sweetness. She peeled the candy. Ate it in slow chews. Her fingers ironed the wrapper back to smoothness.

She crawled under the bed to hide it with her pretties in the love nest. She lifted a loose floorboard and took out a bunch of other candy wrappers held by a bow, then a broken bootlace, a lock of his hair, some wilted wild forget-me-nots, two speckled bird eggs the Holy Ghost had given her, an envelope with *Jewel* printed on it and the head of the President.

She brushed some bugs away. "Old piss ants, you stay 'way from Jewel an' Ruth."

She made a half-circle out of her prizes and let the dawn grow under the bed so she could get a good look up close. She hummed to them. She lost herself in the looking.

The sound of trees falling in the valley brought her back to life. She buried her treasures again and rose. "Wash on Monday," she said. "Iron tomar."

On the path her bare feet had cleared of moss, she lifted one of Jewel's cambric shirts to her face and smelled it. Work sweat and the bark of trees. She liked the mixture.

At the spring she dropped in the clothes, the bar of soap, and then waded in herself. The water swirled cold to cover kneecaps. Before she knew the Holy Ghost haunted the woods, she bathed naked with the clothes; but he might be hiding behind the beech trees that circled the spring. She let her dress tail drop to drink water while she rubbed his shirts, pants and underwear with the yellow soap. "Bake on Wednesday." She baked every day. "Can on Thursday. If 'ey's berries."

The clothes rose up in little puffs. Her fingers poked them down. New ones replaced them.

The water blued her legs. Ached them. She jumped out. "Churn on Friday. If I had a cow." She had Suckie in West Virginia. Electric lights in Kentucky. "Sew on Saturday. Go to meetin' on Sunday." She hadn't spied a steeple since she left Shady Springs.

She knelt to catch the clothes to give them a second soaping. "Come back to me, Jewel," she said to a shirt that tried to get away.

She left the clothes to the fast changing water. By the time she had her morning talk with the Holy Ghost, they would be rinsed, the water sweet for drinking.

She walked past the path's end, into the woods. She would find him. He was everywhere.

He had scared her the first time, down by the sinkhole. He had two dead copperheads hanging from his belt and a live rattler on a wire string. She hadn't screamed when his teeth showed in his yellow beard to say, "What's yore name little girl an' where you from?"

"We's from afar," she had told him. Her name was her own business.

"Who's we?"

"My husband."

Without her asking, he gave his name and occupation. He was a snake hunter. Some he sold alive to the Holiness and to the new snake pits at the filling stations. Others he killed with his hoe and nailed them as portents to the walls of his cabin.

He had pointed to the hollows where Jewel's company was cutting. "Snakes have to leave the hollers. No trees. No stone unturned," he said. "Hell's down there, Heaven here, an' I'm the Holy Ghost."

She had seen pictures of the Father and the Son. She couldn't recollect one of the Holy Ghost. He favored the Father. But littler.

On days when snakes were hiding, he taught her wildflowers: trailing arbutus, johnny-jump-up, slender ladies' tresses. She was partial to them. She wondered if he knew where to find "The Wildwood Flower," but she didn't speak to him unless she was told to. He had proved to be a talker.

"Who's yore daddy, little girl?"

"I'm a woodscolt."

"Who's yore mama, little girl?"

"Vanished."

"Who raised ye, little girl?"

"Ole deaf woman lives in a crib. Then my husband since fourteen. Took me off on a snow-white horse."

"Ain't nobody rides horses since Franklin Delano. Ford pick-ups."

"He did."

"You reckon you's married, little girl?"

"He's pretty."

"Where's ye blood test at, little girl?"

Her blood had not been drawn. The old deaf woman had said, "Where's the papers, honey? Get the papers, honey." But Jewel's foreman married them, without a writing tablet, while they rested on the back of the white horse.

"West Virginia don't take blood." She had turned her face to where the swallows sang.

"You sangle's my Savior."

"West Virginia," she had reminded him.

"When a roll is called up yonder, you better have a set a papers."

Once he led her down the hill to see the temple of the Holy Ghost. She smelled it before she saw it. On the logs of the cabin were wreaths of bleached snake bones. They chimed when he or a breeze brushed them. New ones were nailed through the head, white side outward.

"White bellies brang rain," he said.

She thought of forty days and forty nights.

"Come on in an' I'll give ye a play-pretty," he promised.

She knew better than to enter a strange man's house. Jewel wouldn't even let her look at catalog men in mackinaws. She hurried home. The vines of possum grapes became snakes. The shadows of tree limbs. Roots.

Today he was leaning on his hoe in a huckleberry patch. Nothing dangled from his belt.

"Where you been, little girl?"

"We rest up on the Sabbath," she said.

"Where's ye home, little girl?"

"West Virginia's my home."

"Devil's done got it."

She couldn't say. Jewel wouldn't take her back.

"This world yore home, little girl?"

"We done sawed through two states."

"Ain't but one place worth livin' in."

She waited to hear it.

"'At city 'at lies four-square."

"We ain't been there."

"You gone?"

"We travel on to where 'ey's trees." Tennessee would be next, Jewel said.

"Is yore name printed in a Book a Life?"

"Ruth O'Quin," she said.

"She's dead an' gone."

She pinched a little pucker of skin on her left elbow. It hurt.

"Foller me, little girl."

"Where to?" The snake house had robbed her of a night's sleep.

"Show ye where you buried."

His beard did not smile. His dishwater eyes caught her face and charmed it. She followed. Up a hill, through nettles, down a little valley, up another hill of blue-eyed grass.

At the top, he pointed his hoe at a small graveyard of wasting tombstones.

"Come see," he said.

She approached the grave. A breeze parted the hair of cedars and made a singing sound. His hoe pulled some briars from the face of the marble and hacked them. There underneath a little chipped lamb was "Ruth O'Quin." In print.

A chill shot outward to needle her skin. She knelt to finger the parts of her name, then the lettering and numbers she didn't know. The stone was cold.

"Been dead for years," he said. His eyes watered. She touched the hand that didn't hold the hoe.

"Pore little ghost," he said.

"Hit don't matter," she said, but she felt tears road her face.

With his hoe, the Holy Ghost separated briars on the other graves to look for snakes. The graveyard gave up none. On his way down, he talked to bushes, to trees.

She rested on her grave and hugged her arms against the chill. She tried to think if ghosts could dream, but the whistle of the cedars carried her mind away. It was with the wind. Chasing butterflies.

She slept. Awakened to the wings of a black newsbee. "Yellow for good. Black for bad," she remembered.

She walked home. Over the two hills. Past the spring and the clothes rinsed and hiding at the bottom.

She held onto a porch post and looked down into the valley. Trees fell. "Tim-mmb-burr." Then silence for the birds to sing. Rain crows. Bob Whites. She disremembered to fry Jewel's supper.

Then the sound of the jeep wound around the little dirt road.

She freed the post to catch him in the yard before his boots could shake the porch. He stopped. She saw her face in both his eyes. Two little Ruths. Wild cameos.

"I put my mark on three hundret trees today," he said.

"I'm a ghost," she answered.

He batted her from his eyes. His dinner bucket brushed her dress tail as he walked past her to the house. She turned to watch his stride. She didn't follow.

She heard the dinner bucket clang on the table. She heard a lid lift on an empty pot. Then feet in smaller steps came out. The porch trembled, but did not shake.

"Where's my supper?" One foot had found the ground.

"I'm a ghost." The voice was not her own. It came husky from the grave.

He looked up into tulip trees. He didn't care for ghosts.

"Dead an' buried. For a long time," the voice said.

He raked his hair with both hands and then looked at his palms for new blisters.

"The Holy Ghost showed me my grave today. Up on top the mountain."

"You been talkin' to some crazy Holiness?"

"The Holy Ghost."

"I warned you the first day you rode on my horse." He had. He had told her his shy mama got sanctified in the Holy Spirit and started talking in riddles. He had run away to escape her unknown tongue.

"I'm a ghost. Saw my grave 'is very day."

"Take me to it."

"I shorely will." She passed him and he followed. She had never led before.

By the spring again. He didn't know she washed his clothes in drinking water, but if he saw he didn't say.

The heat of his breath was aginst her neck. Over one hill. She pushed her bare feet fast to beat nightfall. They bruised sawbriars. Scared a snake the Holy Ghost had missed. Over two hills.

When she saw her white stone, a whine parted her lips. It sounded like the cedars talking, but more mournful.

She lay her body down on the grave. The sound stopped, but her breast jerked its sobs against the ground the dews had sprinkled.

She heard his feet circle the grave. His breathing changed from hard to slow.

"O'Quin ain't yore name," he said.

She turned over to see his face bend to hers.

"I was O'Quin when I died."

"O'Quin was yore mama's name. Angels in heaven don't know who your daddy was."

"I answered to O'Quin."

"'At don't matter. You're a Childers now."

"Ain't no Childers neither. Holy Ghost said you didn't mare me."

He lay down beside her and took her hand. She felt the moustaches brush the wetness from her cheeks.

"I will. Swear to God in heaven I will. Tomar at the courthouse. Then you'll be Childers."

Her chin found a resting place in the hollow of his collarbone.

"Can we have our pitcher took?"

"Why yes, baby."

"Together?"

"Like 'is." His chin found her cheek and their faces posed for the whippoorwills.

He quilted the cold from her bones. He didn't spare the ground they rested on.

Then he picked her up in his brave brown arms and carried her down the mountain. The fireflies lighted him the way.

"Tell me a West Virginia dream," she whispered into his ear.

"I dreamt I was ridin' on a snow-white steed an' I come to a road 'at forked two ways. Now the road to the left was where I was headed, but beside the road to the right sat a pretty bird."

"What kind a bird?" she said, as his feet sought solid ground.

"Tiny yeller bird 'at had overworked hits little wangs. I said, 'Would you like to ride on my horse an' rest a spell?' 'I don't mind if I do,' it chirped. I got me down from my horse an' lifted it onto my steed. I jumped on ahind, an' we rode off together."

"Did ye sang to it?"

"Sang 'What's in the Woods for Pretty Bird'."

"Sang it me."

Her lips felt his throat swell, his adam's apple bobbin the notes:

What's in the woods for pretty bird?
What's in the woods for pretty bird?

There's a nest in the woods.
There's a nest in the woods.
Sweet May!

What's in the nest for pretty bird?
What's in the nest for pretty bird?

There's an egg in the nest.
There's an egg in the nest.
Sweet May!

What's in the egg for pretty bird?
What's in the egg for pretty bird?

There's a babe in the egg.
There's a babe in the egg.
Sweet May!

Whose is the babe of pretty bird?
Whose is the babe of pretty bird?

Oh, Jewel, he's the one.
Oh, Jewel, he's the one.
Sweet May!

Her mouth tasted rosin in his hair.
"Sang it me again," she said.
"I shorely will."
His voice silenced the night birds. Filled all the hollows.

Rubygay's Radio

RUBYGAY'S RADIO

When Ole Laid hooved enough sawdust to feel pasture, Rubygay loosened one hand from the rope and waved it at the early morning houses that as yet had only chairs and chickens on their porches. "Fine today," she said low. "An' a great big howdy to you all." Her head ducked the bushes that slapped the truck from both sides of the dirt road.

Brother Rose slid his left hand out the truck window and twiddled his fingers in the rubber crease the door made. Her pointing finger counted ten big black hairs before he grabbed it and then her hand. He scratched three times in her palm to say he hankered her with him, but there was no room in the cab. His wife, Sister Myrtle, scrunched his ribs and nursed his daddy, Uncle Billy, who had whined to ride the back with Rubygay. But she couldn't slow his St. Vitus and also look to the cow. Billy's head swiveled when they took the curves and kept him from winking his tic back at her. Her mama's lap held Rubygay's daddy, though one knee would have served. On smooth stretches her mama craned her neck backwards to spy on Rubygay and the family cow that was to be sacrificed for the lawing.

Brother Rose broke his hold. He required the use of both hands to wheel around Sickle Curve. Rubygay cornered herself in the truck bed so her mama couldn't see and inched her free hand up the velveteen to feel see was it kicking. It was, and the biscuits and Hoover sop she ate for breakfast weren't laying right. Her thumb found the crease of her navel and pushed downward. Ole Laid mourned through her nose.

" 'At cow falls down an' breaks a lag an' I brain ye," her mama's head took all the right truck window to holler.

Rubygay pulled the slack out of the rope and petted Laid's neck. Her mama's head, satisfied, rolled back in.

"Fine today, ole cow," she said. She nodded to an abandoned store. "An' a great big howdy to you all."

She had to hold on tight when the three truck loads of Crabtree witnesses passed to try to get to Grundy first.

The green one had her sister Florie in it, with her husband Dale Crabtree driving. He was Cecil's brother, but bigger. Rubygay and Cecil had made love to Dale's RCA radio through two pairs of shoes she bought with May Apple root.

"Slut," she heard her mama scream. Rubygay couldn't swear which daughter she meant. When her mama heard Florie was going to stand up for Cecil, she picked the pearls out of her Mother pin and sent the spelling back to Florie.

The second truck—black—passed before she could turn glimpse who was in the cab, but a crowd of rowdy boys occupied the bed. They grabbed each others' privates an put thumbs between their first two fingers to play like they had pulled off the nubs of doo-hickies. These they waved to Rubygay. She waved back. Her mama's fist beat shalt-not against the back window.

The third truck she knew best. Red. It belonged to Cecil's daddy, and Cecil had once brushed its gearstick against her thigh. Cecil sat on top of the truck cab to make him look tall. His shirt tail was out and puffing in the wind. On both sides of him stood the two Copperhead Cowboys he made music with.

"Lookie who's on top!" they yelled and pointed guitar and banjo at his mandolin on high.

"Law's gone ride yore ass low," her daddy warned.

Brother Rose tailgated the red and tried to pass left. It hogged the road. Brother Rose tried the right side, but the ditch scotched the wheels and sent Uncle Billy and her daddy feeling for floor pedals. Her mama toppled her flesh out onto the bank and waved son-of-a-bitch through ivy toward the red truck.

Brother Rose stepped down to view the tread and to calm Rubygay's nerves. Ole Laid was the one that trembled.

"Just ye wait, little lady." He held her hand through the slats. "The laws'll hump his back."

Rubygay sweetened a smile, though her breakfast had soured. It was working its way up to her throat.

Brother Rose burnt rubber to rock them out of the ditch and then he floor-boarded to catch the Crabtrees.

They passed the red, and the faces of Sister Rose and her mama turned to show teeth toward Cecil. Billy held his hands to his cheekbones to keep his head steady. Her daddy clutched the knobs on the dashboard.

They overtook the second in one spurt. And when the green slowed down for some chickens in the road, Brother Rose made his arms grow and parted feathers to pass it. They missed going over Big Praetor by a hair.

"Who's on top now?" she heard Brother Rose ask. Nobody answered. Billy and her daddy flung arms for flesh or metal.

The next ten miles they spent overtaking and overtook, on roads cut for mules. She lost the rope and the cow bounced from side to side. Rubygay felt the new dress Billy bought her accept splinters.

On a curve she didn't know, she couldn't churn down her breakfast any longer. Her mouth opened wide and gave what it had over the truck's side.

Nobody noticed. They were relapping, and the Crabtrees were in front. Rubygay wished she was back home molding butter into roses.

They would have won the truck race, but they had to stop at Drill to sell Ole Laid. Only $25.00, though Solomon had topped her and she would come fresh in November.

Without Laid and with a paved road, she could have waved at both sides, but the houses zipped too fast. She counted three twinkling hot dogs and a big biscuit that opened lips to show pickle and a pink piece of meat.

By the time they reached the Courthouse, two hours early, the baby kicked waves into her velveteen. She wanted to say it was hungry, but her mama and daddy had deafened their ears to her voice till she was made an honest woman.

Billy trembled change in his pockets to show he was rich. Before Rubygay could pine to him her need, her mama scurried her inside the gray stone building whose sign didn't twinkle.

They sat through one rape and two non-supports. Her stomach rumbled. Her tongue traced her teeth to play like it was cleaning up after supper. The growls grew. Her daddy's boney knee pushed her left thigh quiet and her mama wedged the other one.

"Rip," her mama whispered.

"Trollop," her daddy said aloud.

"The Court calls the paternity case of Perry Howard against Abner Crabtree." Her name and Cecil's had refused to take the papers.

A crowd of strangers, leftovers from earlier trials, took sides. The three loads of Crabtrees crowded one half, with Cecil's mama and Abner looking lost in the circles. Most of the strangers had to pick her daddy's side. She liked a crowd, but she couldn't turn around to nod to the faces.

Their lawyer—Mr. Viers—and the Crabtree one with swimmy eyes rose to front the man on high, who pulled out his pocketwatch. The three men whispered and frowned. Rubygay wished the Judge would call quitting time, but the clock on the wall said only 11:30.

"The Court calls the plaintiff, Perry Howard, to the stand."

"Mooooo," moaned somebody on the left side. The Judge and lawyers darted their heads for the sound.

"Mooooo."

The Judge took a wooden hammer and waved it. "What is that racket?" he asked.

Nobody told him of Laid or the calf that was supposed to be her wedding gift.

"Moo-ooo-ooo," the crowd said.

"I'll fine ever last one of you for contempt," the Judge threatened.

They swore Perry in. Rubygay tried not to listen. He hadn't had a good word for her in two months.

"A good girl, till she took to settin' up with the Crabtree radio."

Her mind played it was traveling to WSM, Nashville, but her daddy's voice butted in.

"Pickin' got in her blood. Brought on notions."

The Crabtrees laughed. Rubygay started to smile but remembered not to. She looked down at her first pumps. A small dab of green cow manure made longer the left toe. Now that she saw it she could smell it. It fought with the odor of patent leather.

"Knowed only hymns till 'at radio come to Copperhead. Started breakin saucers an' hummin' sin."

The RCA broke her maidenhead, but she hadn't told on it. While Roy Acuff was tuning up, Cecil positioned her on his lap and whispered to the back of her head, "Less me an' you take daddy's truck an' the Grad Ole Opry for a honeymoon." He mistook her nod, and before the fiddle chased the night train to Memphis, Cecil was working without a raincoat on her insides.

"Why didn't you put a stop to her galavantin'?" Cecil's lawyer crossed.

"Did. I shot the god-damn radio."

The radio had turned him from God. While Dale was off

logging and Florie in her garden, her daddy had slipped into their front room and wasted salvation and two shells on the oak. The batteries played on, but not on Rubygay.

The lawyers didn't ask Perry any longer.

"The Court calls Bessie Howard to the stand."

Her mama trembled waves into her darkest dress. Her neck crept into its high collar.

"Go see what can ye do," her daddy said.

Bessie took tiny steps. She stopped twice in a path she would have taken in two strides if it led to a corn field. She wiped her brow. Somewhere a baby cried. Her mama held her heart that never skipped.

Bessie Howard was her name. On Copperhead she lived. But she balked when they shoved the Bible beneath her chin. Wagged no with the flesh flaps of her throat.

"Swear not atall," she said. Over the supper table, she had wavered in her testimonies. Rubygay was a whore. Rubygay was a good milker. Rubygay's neck should be unjointed. Rubygay's butter never patterned a hair. Now the Lord turned her silent.

"Mrs. Howard, you can't stand up for your daughter if you don't swear on the Bible," Mr. Viers told her.

"Bible says swear not atall." Bessie couldn't read, but her mind stuck to what Scriptures it heard.

"If you don't take the oath, you can't have a say," the Judge said.

"Not atall."

"Witness dismissed."

Bessie's eyes caught Rubygay's and shied them. Rubygay spread her thighs for her mama's pinch.

Sister Myrtle Rose, who had passed by Rubygay's feet at a footwashing, now climbed to the stand to tell how good Rubygay was. Rubygay was hungry.

"Who can find a virtchus woman?" Myrtle was recollecting. The same question had been asked over Ole Lady Bostic's corpse.

"Her price is 'bove rubies."

"Aman," a few strangers helped Brother Rose to say. Rubygay didn't say. She didn't know her verses.

"She girdles her loins. Her merchandise is good...."

The Judge was trying to flag her down, but Sister Rose closed her eyes, held both sides of her curls against the headache the trip had given her, and tongued out her say. Rubygay couldn't catch it all.

"She is not 'fraid a the snow."

Rubygay did all the winter chores so the young could go to school.

"Put the fruit in her hands, an' let her works praise her at the gates."

She reckoned Sister Rose meant the Pearly.

The Judge was curious too. "What do rubies and gates have to do with the paternity of that girl's baby?"

"Jedge not lest ye be jedged," Myrtle opened her eyes to remind him.

"Aman," Brother Rose said so loud he woke up his daddy Billy, who aimed his tic in Rubygay's direction.

"Druther sit at the feet a Jesus 'n dwell in the court a Pilate."

"Dismiss that woman. She rails," the Judge hammered.

"Sister Rose, you can step down," Mr. Viers told her.

"Render onto Caesar that which is Caesar's." She pointed toward hell. She rose from the witness chair and pulled at both sides of her hem to make sure she wasn't sweatstuck at the flanks. Then her hands remembered her hair.

"Next," the Judge said and looked mean at his watch.

"I'd like to call Reverend Bobby Lee Rose to the stand."

Rubygay's stomach stopped its churning. The baby's feet rested. Brother Rose, tall and pretty, made every step to the stand sound his power.

"Last chanct, rip," her mama whispered.

"Trollop," her daddy said.

At first Brother Rose wouldn't swear to nothing-but-the-truth-so-help-you-God. The Judge flapped his black wings and frowned.

"I'm not aquinted with 'at book," Brother Rose told the clerk with a limber Bible.

"Witness dismissed," the Judge beat out.

"If hit ain't been chopped a-pieces, I'll swear."

The clerk handed Brother Rose the book and he Bible-drilled it fast. He petted it with a right hand so big it almost covered the black.

"Name, address, occupation," Mr. Viers said.

"Reverend Bobby Lee Rose. I dwell with my daddy, Uncle Billy Rose, up on Lick Creek, an' I preach the Gospel Untampered With."

"How well do you know Miss Rubygay Howard?"

"I'm aquinted with her soul."

Rubygay wished she could leave her all on the altar to go home eat.

"Tell the Court about her character."

"Under me, she taken the Lord Jesus Christ as her personal."

Rubygay had been saved each summer since thirteen, but Brother Rose sanctified her, filled her with the Holy Ghost.

Brother Rose's eyes glazed for delivery. His throat swelled. "She was sangin' 'Fly 'Way Ole Glory' at the sinner call an' the spirit fell on 'er an' she fainted out dead. We cared 'er out to let the night air fan 'er."

"She craves night air," someone on Cecil's side said, but Brother Rose was in gear.

"I had to push up an' down on 'er ribs an' brang 'er 'round. She danced for Jesus on the snowy ground. Next Sunday I baptized 'er in the Johnson Hole. She didn't choke, an' I helt 'er down long for to see."

She had been afraid she'd spurt and prove a hypocrite, but his hand took mouth and nose and she came up treading mud for Jesus.

"How would you estimate her character?"

"One of the best hit's been my ministry to know."

"Would you call her a loose woman?"

"Not by a stretch. Anybody 'at faints for the Lord like 'at is saved."

Rubygay had become famous that summer for fainting. The corners of her mouth smiled out the memory. Her mama didn't catch it.

"Your witness," Mr. Viers said.

Cecil's lawyer paced up and down the space between the two seats on high and the low rows for listeners. Rubygay inched her to forward, flipped it over, and smeared the dab of green on the floor.

"Mr. Rose, what is your church?"

"Church Of The Lord Jesus Christ Be With You All Aman."

"Aman," Sister Rose agreed.

"Where's its headquarters?"

"Heavan Up Above."

The lawyer grinned at the Judge and stroked a bald chin and swam his eyes first at the preacher, then at Rubygay. Rubygay pretended she had Spearmint wallowing around in her mouth. She chewed at him.

"When first did you preach at Perry Howard's house up on Copperhead?"

"Last Febaworry."

"How far gone is Rubygay?"

"Lordy, I can't hardly know."

"Report of medical science is six months plus." A doctor had kneaded her flesh when she got her blood tested.

"Only doctor I know is Jesus."

Bessie clapped her hands. Sister Rose spasmed her curls. Uncle Billy's head looked like it was listening to the radio.

"August from February equals six months," reckoned the lawyer.

Mr. Viers waved his hands at the Judge, but he was smiling and missed the signs.

"Did you ever loosen Rubygay's brassiere?"

"Onct. When she's fainted out. In sight a God an' man."

"Why did you play with her underclothes?"

"Was to help the circulation. We thought she's dead."

"Did you pull her slippers off?"

"At a footwarshin' I did." Brother Rose had crossed over from the men's side when his wife wouldn't wash even one of Rubygay's feet.

"Did you tickle her feet?"

Cecil's side whistled. The Judge didn't pound.

"Warshed 'em. As my Jesus beckoned."

"That Howard woman was full of child, was she not?"

"Mary Magdalene," Brother Rose preached. "Woman at the Well."

Cecil's lawyer whispered to the Judge. His mouth left the Judge's ear and spread. The Judge's cheeks puffed round for grin.

"The witness may step down," the Judge ruled.

Brother Rose's eyes danced they had just started, but it was Cecil's turn.

His mama and daddy wouldn't come forth. The lawyer had to start with Ray, Cecil's youngest brother. His hands fought for pockets as he swaggered up to swear.

Rubygay's stomach and the baby told her new hunger. Her ears remembered how fatback sizzled when it fried.

Ray picked at the buttons on his shirt and lied. "I stomped on 'er foot an' she didn't budge."

He flirted with brimstone by swearing he handed her a Moon Pie to let him peep Ole Santy.

"Did you have carnal knowledge of this little girl?" Mr. Viers crossed him.

Ray grinned. "Takes both arms to gird 'er."

Rubygay's finger found her naval through the new and old layers. Her mama grabbed her hand and dug its palm for blood.

"Answer my question!"

"What does hit mean?"

"Did you know her biblically?"

Ray changed his hands to his back pockets and shifted his left hip so low it seemed out of socket.

"Did you...?"

"Did ye saw ye off a little piece?" somebody yelled.

Her daddy muttered abominations and with his little haunches pushed her toward her mama. "Rip," her mama said, and prized her back.

The Judge stood up and scolded with his mallet.

"No. But I got my hands up under 'er dress tail an' skinned 'ese offin 'er." From inside his shirt Ray pulled forth a pair of mail-order step-ins, black with baby roses.

"Exhibit A," their lawyer said.

"My youngen don't wear 'em drawyers," her mama jumped up to swear. She trembled and shook the row of seats when she fought back down.

"Order. Order. Order!" the Judge commanded.

Rubygay wished for COD, Chicago.

Talby Lockhart came to stand up for Cecil. He told about rubbing up against her on the back porch of Trilla Bostic's wake. Rubygay wanted to tell his honor that Cecil said Talby didn't have no doo-hickey to speak of.

The crowd quieted when Dale Crabtree made his overall pants whisper starch all the way to the stand. Dale was as pretty as Brother Rose. He used to let her play "giddy-up, giddy-up" on his full lap when Florie was in the garden.

"My sis-in-law," he was saying. "Cecil, he's my brother."

"Cecil and Rubygay did most of their courting at your house is that right?"

"Come to listen to the Grand Ole Opry." He forgot the *Gospel Fires* on some Sunday nights. But she kept her legs crossed when God was on.

"Did Cecil behave?"

"They sat in our big armchair an' listened to the pickin'. Ever Saturday night when they's no meetin'."

She sat on Cecil's lap, he claimed eyesore and Florie blew out the lamp to save his sight and kerosene. He plied Rubygay just right, and they made love with her on top and him, little, nussing and neither breathing hard. Her dress tail could have told them if their eyes hadn't been aimed upward at the radio, and when their heads did nod down, she tapped her shoes to the music. Except for Ernest Tubb and "Take Me Back and Try Me One More Time." It was so pretty she froze. Then the fiddles fanned her feet back into flurry.

"Did you ever step out and leave them alone?"

"Me or Florie or Raynelle was always in the room."

"Who is Raynelle?"

"Florie her little sister. Rubygay's too."

"Is she here?"

"Too young to swear."

Her daddy made Raynelle go with them, but she closed her eyes to lip-trace the songs. When Rubygay and Cecil hugged home from Dale's or meetings, Raynelle ran ahead and aimed the flashlight backwards, till they caught up, to see that Cecil wasn't free with his hands. But Rubygay and Cecil learned to play at the blind side.

"Cecil was honorable then?"

"Said hardly a word. Just listened to the music."

She heard her daddy's anger gurgle in his throat. He stood

up and boxed the hot air with the little knots of his fists. " 'At hellfired radio. Hit's the cause."

"Radio ain't got no god-damn pecker," Dale answered.

Rubygay laughed with the others that it didn't. Her mama's hand burnt her lips back into frown. The Judge hammered and choked, hammered and hollered.

Rubygay squeezed her thighs to their valley and thought of Uncle Dave Macon's Cluck Ole Hen, of Roy Acuff's Great Speckled Bird. Both stewed with dumplings.

Florie sat in the chair and played with the circle hair-do a round rat made. Rubygay tried to close some of her out.

"Cecil's honest as the day is long. A worker, too. Cares me my water an' fires my stove."

Cecil slept at Florie's when Dale was away logging. Florie forgot the joints he rubbed with liniment. His hands always smelled of sweet herbs.

"He's on the shy side, but he can make a mandolin talk. Just a baby, he is."

Florie's liver was white and made her barren and she babied Cecil.

"He's not reached his growth. Ain't filled out yet."

Cecil was two more than Rubygay, but his inches had stopped on him at twelve.

Mr. Viers faced Florie.

"I won't say a word to harm my sister's name, but she draws men. Like flies to honey."

Some lips smacked. Others went buzz.

"Would you say your flesh and blood is a whore?" Mr. Viers asked.

"She never could keep her hands out from under the kevers."

Then Cecil sidled down the aisle like a banty addled on the right side. Rubygay looked him in the eye, but he turned red and aimed his vision upward.

In his testimony he counted only one time—the worst—when some eavesdropping boys watched them through the cracks of her daddy's springhouse and then ran told everybody Cecil was churning her butter. That day her daddy whipped her with a hoe handle, and her mama, once she lifted Rubygay's dress tail, studied up ways to make the baby drop.

Tote lard cans of wash water. Galvanized tubs of apples.

Drink a pint of turpentine.

Rubygay just belched for a week.

"When did you have relations in the springhouse?"

"June meetin'. First Sunday in June. Graveyard meetin'. We outrun Raynelle an' hid in the spranghouse."

"That was two months ago."

"Come Sunday."

"And you never had carnal knowledge of Ruby before the June meeting?"

"Not never. Not after neither."

"Your witness." The lawyer looked at Rubygay, not at Mr. Viers.

Rubygay glanced at what was hers till her daddy went wild and called it runt and shot Dale's radio.

Mr. Viers unfrogged his throat and tried to put a spell on Cecil. Leveled his eyes on his, but Cecil batted him out.

Mr. Viers told all the places, except the radio. The dates Rubygay couldn't recollect. She could tell the time a clock said, but when she looked at a calendar she saw only the Dionne Quintuplets.

In the elderberry bushes, the sinkhole in the holly patch, the springhouse more than once, the ditch at Sickle Curve walking home from a revival, standing upright drawing water from the well. Every place except the big chair at Dale's, nearly every Saturday night for two pairs of shoes.

"You never promised to marry this little lady?"

"Swear to God."

"Never said you'd make her an honest woman?"

"Pond my honor."

"Never said you'd like to daddy her babies?"

"Stack a Bibles."

"Puss-gut runt," her daddy screamed. "Sawed-off sumbitch."

"Step outdoors an' say it to my face," Cecil threatened.

Perry didn't wait for the outside. He gave a leap and a runego and scaled the perch to wrestle at Cecil's windpipe. Brother Rose bellowed verses and brought blood to the noses of Ray and Talby. Her mama mistook Rubygay for a Crabtree. Started slapping her. Rubygay lifted her arms to take the bee stings meant for her head.

"Call the laws!" somebody yelled.

"This is the law," Sister Rose answered. "Man's law." She rose to show them God's.

Blue shirts came from nowhere to try to part the sides.

The Judge banged his hammer and deemed Cecil a free man. Pounded out jail and court costs for her daddy.

"Moooo," the left crowd went.

"Who's on top now?" Florie prissed. Bessie left Rubygay's head to help Sister Rose double up on Florie. They yanked the rat from her hair to show the world she was balding.

The lawyers were prized out. The Judge flapped his wings and parted curtains in the back of his high chair and was swept away.

The laws lifted her daddy dangling from the room. Her mama sweated after. Screamed for justice. Slapped the heads of two blue shirts with her purse.

"Recess! Recess!" the clerk called.

Rubygay remembered school yard. Dodgeball.

"Clear the courtroom." The laws fanned the hot air with their clubs.

Sister Rose held her curls. Uncle Billy let his head dance its way out. Brother Rose offered an arm and a clean handkerchief for Rubygay's eyes, but they were dry.

While her mama cried to the Judge and jailer, Rubygay and Brother Rose, Sister Myrtle and Uncle Billy sat across the street in the New Dixie Cafe and ate them a snack. Rubygay ordered two footlong hot dogs, with buttermilk to chase them down.

Billy's legs trembled under the table and shook the velveteen.

"Less me an' you get mared," he whispered.

She chewed.

"Buy ye some step-ins," he promised.

Brother Rose rested his coffee to help his daddy move her. "You can sang with us," he said. He spread his big hands on the table. Palmed them up for her to see.

"Wife's place is in a home," Sister Rose said. She played with her headache Co-Cola hadn't cured.

"What ye say?" Billy asked.

Sister Rose started to say, but Brother Rose's eyes scotched her tongue.

"How 'bout it, honey?" Brother Rose pleaded. "I'd be ye son." He raised his right hand and babychucked her chin.

"Don't wont no in-law hussy for my mama an' my granny," Sister Rose huffed. "No whorehoppin' in my Christian home."

"My house it is," Uncle Billy shook at Myrtle. "Truck, too."

Rubygay swirled the glass to gather the last of the buttermilk. Lifted it high so the drops could slide.

"Buy ye a radio," Billy aimed at Rubygay.

The glass was dry. She nodded.

She already had her certificate for pure blood, in case the judge said Cecil, and Uncle Billy's didn't take long once the nurses spied a vein. Brother Rose married them in the truck bed, while they leaned against the new Philco Upright. Then he took Myrtle's forbidden lipstick to write the wedding on the truck doors.

They found Perry distracted in the middle of Main Street,

daring coal trucks to run him down. Bessie was keeping up from the sidewalk.

When Brother Rose stopped traffic to gather him, Perry was too rattled to tell his fate, but Bessie cried a lien on Solomon the bull. Uncle Billy quavered he'd buy Laid back.

Brother Rose figured the bride and groom should sit in the cab with him, but Rubygay wouldn't risk the radio. She and Billy rode the back with it and, after Drill, with Laid. The music fought static, but once they passed electricity, she found the last two verses of Ernest Tubb and "Walkin' the Floor Over You."

Twice she slapped a palm one-two-three on the cab to make Brother Rose brake for Billy to tremble out some change for candy. She gave everybody a gum drop, two jelly beans.

When they bounced up the holler at Copperhead, night had not yet fallen. Brother Rose bore down on the horn to help out the radio. Houses emptied to their porches to read "Just Mared" on both doors of the truck and to see Billy and Rubygay holding hands to circle the radio, with Laid nustling at the knot for entry.

"Who's on top now?" her mama hollered above the noise as they passed Dale Crabtree's empty porch.

"Who's on top now?" she asked again when they passed Abner's house.

But Rubygay, when she saw Cecil peeping through a curtain, freed a hand to wave. Waved it and said, "Fine today, an' a great big howdy to you all."

The Quilt

THE QUILT

As a prize for reaching accountability, the five girls got quilts to warm their marriage beds; the four boys got bull calves. The bulls' story can be told in auctioneer haste, since the fate of a bull calf is almost always a cocked gun.

But quilts. They hold the sweet must of a summer's mildew; they remember November and the chill that makes the knee caps crawl toward the chin. But with such bedhuggers, a winter's feet might forget to scar with crusty swirls the morning's frozen linoleum.

Quilts. Sears and Wards and Aldens devoted one thick glossy page and one or two toilet-paper thins to them. Aunt Ida, who had gone to normal and could paint the hint of a Japanese dragon on a cup, quilted comforters that would have made Joseph rip off his coat of many colors to lie down under her rainbows. She and Lottie, the hired girl of 40 who stayed with Granddaddy and Uncle Odin while Ida ran the P.O. and the store, made doilies that defied the laws of gravity, their starched waves aiming to tickle in wedding-cake grace the lacy beard of God. They made white crocheted bedspreads that would have snowed over the state of Rhode Island.

But their quilts. Their Butterfly, winging its technicolor way through the threads of a cotton cocoon; their Horse Shoe that could have clopped only through the gates of Troy; their Bird of Paradise, which twinkled its message in tiny squares and tried to look like a turkey with an inflamed tail; they not knowing that the phoenix is an illusive bird and burns its shape only on those minds that have spread their gray for branding — I saw it, when I slept there, as Roy Acuff's Great Speckled Bird that would swoop down like a buzzard blued into beauty to sleep me through green pastures to that mansion in the sky; their Sunflower that had never nodded its head with the sun to the West, but burned its erect yellows on a background of green so green that the saps of spring would never have claimed acquaintance; their Nine Diamonds — a geometry sufficient for God at quitting time on the fourth day — diamonds within diamonds, triangles within triangles, without a hint that thread puckered them together. And other quilts whose very names covered their daily loves and cares, from November through March: Wild Rose Bouquet, Poplar Leaf, Sugar Bowl. If the pattern hinted of more permanent woes, of Old Maid's Puzzle or of the gauzed ropes of the Spiderweb, its artistry was so cunning you forgot the fingers of the Fates curve downward from the weight of thimbles and you thought, instead, of the crispness of Penelope's calluses to the sea-cracked hands of Odysseus.

Mama's patterns were not so exotic. The fabric had been faded from the chemistry of sweat, distorted by the muscles that pushed against the weave. She stitched one Jacob's Ladder, but there was not enough color to approximate the upper rungs toward heaven. Her Drunkard's Path was as drab as its theme — the leftover husks of those who had indeed threaded the night in uncertain, but necessary, stitches. When Mama had collected enough patches of color for creation and when the snows froze her fingers to forget the earth, her first and last love — she tried her hands at quilting the metaphors they had touched: the Gate Latch, the Anvil, and the Churn Dasher. These handrubbed subjects would render a rough grace, like the buckshot artistry of wild mustard bloom or the splintered symmetry of a new rail fence.

But Mama's comforters were usually Friendships, those sewn by women who passed from house to house in snow time to exchange whatever cotton or wool wear had made useless. When things could not be held together with tooth-resistant thread, the women reverted to twine; and when twine would not draw the curtains on flesh, the fabric could, in clear conscience, be microspasmed into little squares of experience, which when barn-builded with the artistry of fingers and the rheum of eyes, could be resurrected in a Friendship quilt.

From the ceiling of the "big" room hung upside-down question marks, metal claws that supported the wooden frame around which the women sat. First came the lining of chopsack dyed with Rit, but never so colored that the blunt heads of advertising cows or the pink jowls of Purina hogs did not shine through, like photo negatives that the sun has peeped and blistered. Onto the dyed chopsack, carpet-tacked to the frame, fell the snowy bed of store-bought cotton, or of frayed outing flannel when the times were not fluffy enough for cotton. Then the pinchers of the wooden frame caught the pattern, spread it, and the room was suddenly fanned into fullness. While some of the women stitched tomorrow's pattern, others sat around the swaying table of fragile cloth and sewed until it shrank from the roll of the frame sticks and the accomplishment of their needles to an area where only four had elbow room for sewing, and then until only two could stitch and, finally, till only one could bite the No. 50 thread and tie the quilt's umbilical cord.

I remember the low, almost whispered, allowings of the women as the movement of their wrists and the clicking of their thimbles made sleight-of-hand an art. It was like watching Press Fletcher harness a horse without looking at its back, or blind Orvil Compton, who knew how hands could fumble yards away for a horseshoe ringer.

The ones who shared with Mama their faded scraps were as different as the material they brought for the pattern.

Aunt Viney Nuckols. Called Aunt long before her parts dried up on her. Aunt Viney would roll her eyes upward towards the caller. Her mouth would thread its way to a sad dangle and then twitch out the stitches of a whimper, "Jimmy, 'lowed I died last night an I did too." Aunt Viney had neuralgia before the labels on patent medicines got it. Her mail-order glasses, one lens knocked out, gave her right eye a strange plumpness. She had arthritis till quilting time came. She punished from those rare symptoms that women sometimes smelled of but never mentioned, except in whispers, as "female trouble," a rich smell of red dishrags steeped in menstrual flow and hidden to age in old boxes. Later I learned it was the egg that would not rot on her. Just stayed in, hardening to a yearly break.

"Jimmy 'lowed I died last night an I did too."

"Weeell I sware."

"Sa pity."

"Sa shame."

"A body don't know."

"Well I do say."

"He calls ye when ye time comes."

"At's a way I figure."

"Pale as a hant, an Jimmy 'lowed I died last night an I did too."

Tory, whose very name spelled Republican, but whose hands smelled of butter. The movement of her joints seemed greased with the yellow brain a milking gives when it's churned. She was the wife of Ezra Hess, a Hardshell preacher who spread the Word at meetings, funerals and wakes. Tory had seeped up his texts, but not his screaming delivery. (Once he got so happy in the Lord he threw his shoes and socks down Cherry Mountain and danced barefooted, his right hand cupped over his right ear to get the steps the spirit whispered him.) When the quilting talk turned to the times, Tory's low voice, distorted slightly by the pipe that rested around moist bubbles in the corner of her mouth, would melt the idols of Mammon.

"Seasier fur camel to crawl through the eye ufa needle an fur a rich man tenter the kingdom a heaven."

"Swat it says."

"Bible don't lie."

"Only true story ey is."

"Camels big han't dey?"

"Tallern trees."

"Aw shaw!"

"Yes mam. Ey's big brown fellers."

"Got some purshin to do, don't he?"

"Hit ain't never a rich man got der nohow."

"Not hardly."

"Bible. Hit don't lie."

"At's what Jimmy says an I do too."

Omie Tiller, whose cud of tobacco often made her a mimer in the work of mouth and hands. She swallowed the juice without grimace. She always came when she had a dose of Pinkham's Compound and wasn't, therefore, crazy. When she did come, she could sew the fire out of a quilt. She'd shift the cud of tobacco, a movement unimpaired by the grave markers of teeth, and allow the speed of her chewing to say that she was happy that eyes had seen what hands could do, given the chance to touch something.

"Saw red bird churnin up snow this morn. Be early sprang."

"Weeell."

"Aunt Rhodie allis allowed such."

"Do declare."

"Hit just got hits feet to dancin an hits wings to flappin and just spread dat snow."

"A red bird churnin up at snow?"

"A sight to see."

"Just churnin up at snow."

"A red bird."

Hazel Johnson, who brought Zack to lie with me under the quilt, a position that dictated a change when the frame was rolled inward. Hazel talked of Billy Nolley Peck, of Raw Bones and Bloody Skull, of Haskew Fletcher who chopped up little girls and cut off the ribbons of little boys. With my lungs as an excuse for being home from school, I sat and listened to the fingers and smelled the cake dough in Zack's diaper and heard the bloody tales of Hazel. They made my eyes stretch for new circles of wonder, but the Friendship insulated my fears. Tory only grunted in Christian disbelief. The clicking of Mama's needle on thimble allowed that it was possible, but not likely.

"Haskew Fletcher done torim up inother school youngen."

"Says who?"

"Darnil he hear it out on the road yestidy."

"What name she of?"

"Darnil can't know — just hear tell he torer open an threwer in Dismal Branch. Say eyes rolled back white an biggern banty eggs."

"Reckon?"

"Ain't no tellin."

"This world an' one more."

"Senough fur any uf us."

"Darnil say getim a boy next. Cutser dohickies off an eatsem like Viennie sausage."

"Do you reckon?"

"I can't rightly know."

And Hazel would go back to chewing her second-hand gum. She'd push out old gum with a spoon and sprinkle the rubber dough with new sugar and then roll it up for another chewing.

If they ever spelled their fingers, it was to delouse Marie Newberry, whose head bore a burden of bugs knitting at her hair. I remember their joy at 206, when Tory announced that number of cracked ones. And then the hands, juiced on the fat depravity of head lice, went back to clicking.

Marie had no children, but she always talked about pregnancies.

"Hear tell Arizonie Dibble's spectin."

"Ow many's at make?"

"Leben, if ye count dem two pore twins."

"Ey's two cordin Jesus."

"Soon be to accountability an ain't never set footun the floor."

"Hear tell Arizonnie diapers em."

"Has to. Can't help emselves."

"Wonder thisen have twelve toes?"

"All has, I reckon."

"Twelve fangers too."

"Mark a the beast."

"We'll understand hit better by an by."

Livy MacFarland, whose two sons Jake and Talbert had gone to the war, one saved, the other dead. Livy would sing in a low voice, as if it didn't really matter, that we should remember her Jake died for the "redwhiteanblue." And sometimes she'd sing "Oh Where Is My Wonderin Boy Tonight?" that brought a strange hoarseness to their voices and a patterned pause, as if their wind pipes had caught an unchewed bite of apple and held it for flavor halfway down.

"Body's gotta bear up."

"Seeim agin in at golden city Four-Square."

"Circle won't be broken the sky, Lord, in the sky."

"Sgot a home in Beulah Land."

"Outshines the sun."

"Some glad mornin."

"When is life is ore."

The thimbles always got frantic when Livy sang. Lucie Colley even stabbed her finger once and didn't notice until somebody saw the drops of blood tracking the white thread, but Lucie never said much of anything. She was the youngest of the quilters, nineteen but fifty, and Nola and Mable remember her from Presley School where she ate her snot buggers. And though I can't recollect ever seeing her actually do it, I'll bank on their being right. Her needle-aiming finger rose between stitches to flick ever so lightly her nose, on either side, and returned to her mouth again. When I was in the primer, I somehow confused it with the lick a finger makes when it turns the pages of a new book. But education makes you see things that aren't there, that couldn't be there in a year of Sundays.

Berthie Bostic, with a goiter that waltzed with the needle three feet away. She didn't say much either. Her neck, with a watermelon wag, told you what was happening, just as Uncle Jake Tiller's marrow told you of rain and snow. Berthie wagged her approval, not the way hands clap in horizontal fannings, but with a slight rise of the Adam's apple and then a flip-flip of her ten-pound growth — the way a coffee pot simpers that it's glad you're up. When she was displeased, if mouths turned to Hoover Times, her goiter tranquiled like the bowl of a wicker basket that snakes sometimes rise from to the flag of a flute.

"Pretty patch a green is my Clairissie. Her mail-order dress. Saved a piece for all eleben."

"Slike sprang."

"Couldn't take the gray waters a Dismal. Fell part aftern she's baptized."

"Sa new green — color of lettuce."

"Help the blacks an blues."

"Nothin like a little color in a Friendship."

"Swat I allis said."

Rubygay Howard, who didn't come often, for her fingers I later learned had other work, brought with her all the whispers that womankind has laryngitized to. Rubygay, who after fainting for the

Lord at a meeting at her daddy's, had been found greeting the aroused extension of Cecil Crabtree in their daubed springhouse, churning butter that was already molded into pattern, upsetting buttermilk that had used up its germs and lay dormant in whey. Although the others' eyebrows would dance first in indignation, their eyes always aimed upwards toward a smile, and even Mama, now and then, would let her high voice drop an octave to warble about Rubygay's contribution to the strange fabric of a Friendship quilt.

"Good service up on Copperhead last Satidy night. Six shouted. I fainted three times. Had to care me out, let the snow fall on my face. Thought I'sa goner."

"Who cared ye?"

"Brother Rose. He taken off his red mackinaw an spread it over-inme. Picked me up like a baby an yelled fur a path to the night air."

"Ow long's ye out?"

"Lordy I don't know. Brother Rose he give me some First Aid."

"What's at?"

"Purshin uppindown on my ribs. Got a life backinme so's I could sang 'Fly 'Way Ole Glory.'"

"Nobody kin sang 'Fly 'Way' like you."

"Lordy I know it."

Roxie Penley, who had the blood of the Savior even in her water and, therefore, could not deem the tan juice useless. Roxie, her back was so straight it dared the body waist down to give her the lie. Her furry mole above the lip seemed to prove the Mark of the Beast she babbled about, while her hands turned cold gingham into future warmth. In the summer Roxie was a caution, for she changed religion with the drop of a tithing hat, but when the cold set in, her denomination set in, and she needled it home to the cloth and to the faces of the bodies a knee-nudge away. She was most fun when the snakehandlers got her, for they charmed her in

September when God usually runs dry in the mountains until the snow melts in April, and everybody thought she was bringing hibernating copperheads clinging to the denim of her knapsack. But Roxie only brought the snakes of her mind.

"Talked to a Lord God a Hosts last night. Got in touch with God. Turned a radio on."

"Weeell."

"Yessirree. Had us a long talk."

"Don't say?"

"Say I do."

"Weell do declare."

"Put my hand ona radio, way preacher on *Gospel Fire* told me to, an juice ufem batteries made purple mallberrries crawl uppin-down my spine."

"Whade say?"

"Said time's drawin nigh. Said ain't no usinto put out a garden come sprang. Trumpet's gone blow. Time be no more."

"What is to be will be."

"Gone put me outsum taters soons signs in bowels."

"En come angurns an lettuce."

"Nothin like a good bait a angurns an lettuce."

"An graveled taters."

"Lord God a Hosts I know ain't calculatin on no sprang."

That was what the Friendships covered. Before the winter sky frowned darkness, the women rose to walk the one-to-five miles home, thinking perhaps of spring when green could be yanked from the ground. Every winter each house was enriched by at least one Friendship, and in my third through seventh winters I followed Mama to all their houses and sat neath the quilting frames with the other children and listened to the low allowings of the quilters.

But the Friendships couldn't take very long the moths of summer, not even the half-hot airs of springtime. The thread would not hold; the squares had been mishandled or torn. Soon we forgot to look at the rough wools and denims of a communal past. If we did look, we saw that the fingers of mountain women, like those of the three Fates, are inexorably faithful in the lulling click of thimbles on material that the sweet air of decay learns to whistle its lament through.

When the quilts did hold together, Mama would tell us their stories on a rainy day when Daddy's wire fencing invited death by lightning or when the ground so mudded that it too would rest from the hacks of our hoes.

"Tory's Sundaygotomeetin dress."

"Omie's print she bought day she found at hen's nest with 21 eggs in it."

"Marie's green blouse."

"Livy—Jake his overall pants at, when he died, wouldn't fit Talbert."

"Lucie Colley her first wake dress."

"Berthie's last Friendship square, bless her soul. Her outin princess slip."

"Roxie's flowerdy she got dat year Seven-Days Adventists passed through an turnder Sunday into work day. Prayed all Satidy an sweat uppa storm on Sabbath."

"Aunt Viney's pank weddin dress. Safore youens knowder. Pretty's a pup an flashy."

"Red velveteen Rubygay wore to courtday when judge 'lowed Cecil didn't hav't make hern honest woman."

"At's Hazel—britches her Darnil wore."

Then the Friendships disappeared. A one—to—five mile change came over people. Before electric light bulbs hung like the noses of nightmares from yellow cords, the women had a duty to make a Friendship quilt, but when night could be day with the first commandment flicker of a finger, things changed. Folks sat under those green-yellow coils and looked at walls they never before thought were dirty, but now they saw that flies do hover over August slops and then settle the period of their bowels on walls. The catalog pages that had squared the rooms in frames of impossible promise suddenly peeled, like the skin of a snake long past a July shed, and folks bought sheetrock against the shame. In what they thought was progress, they covered the Hoover wallpaper with the gray white of tombs and then, closed in by the fierceness of pallor, they smeared the white with what catalogs could provide — blues that only unborn robins should know, the pinks of the skinned gizzards of geese. But like the pages of a leisurely read book, it all turned, and Mama made what she called her Friendship alone — sometimes at night when her red nerve medicine didn't work for her and she needed something to hold onto to keep her hands quiet, but mostly at day when we were all at school or away up North working.

For us her new Friendships were more compelling. They became a picture book of our own particular past, not of the times when people rode only horses and wore clothes the catalogs didn't show. After Roscoe and Daddy died, she gave up quilting and the Bible. We gave her a purebred Collie pup and a TV to make Christmas seem nightly. When we would come home on vacation or for the funerals of Pasco and Cotton, we'd hear her talk of the latter-day Friendships. At night we'd shed a comfortable tear on sheets we had bought her with Green Stamps, sheets washed and spread especially for us, sometimes hoarded five years before their plastic pouches were torn. Her gnarled fingers wished once more to comfort the beds of babies who had been reared to lie on harsher material, but who were lying down now on the satin pillows and ruffles of caskets. By rising early to fry up breakfast, we six living told her we knew her hands didn't have the thimble, didn't have even the curling nerves to tell when the electric stove eyes were on. But her eyes, rolling in wonder toward eighty, told us the story of quilts that had been stitched stronger than death against the moths, the mildew, and the rains that tease marble headstones.

We lie on the floor again, without a storm, and take a quilt for her to recount the pieces. Her fingers travel the map of an Anvil or a Friendship to point out what covered us in times gone by.

Wish Book

WISH BOOK

Brownie's laziest bark always announced her, with Buck in her arms and two skinny dogs and a sore-eyed cat following. She never knocked, but we could hear the bones of her dogs find scratching space on the kitchen porch.

If Daddy was home, he rose from the table to go sit by his silent radio in the big room. But Mama never turned anyone away. And Maudie didn't beg. She just stood on the porch till Mama fanned the screen door to say, "Come eat with us."

"I ain't a bit hongry," she'd say. But she came inside to sit by the cookstove to watch us eat.

"Give Buck some bread," Mama would say.

Maudie chewed and then slipped little wads past the sores on Buck's lips. If there was any left, she would hide it in the pocket of her chop-sack dress that spelled COW CHOW, PIG STARTER. She couldn't spare for bleach, and the many boilings in her iron pot had taken only the bolder blacks.

When we had work, Maudie tried to help.

If it rained, we played Wish Book. Or Fortune.

Mama liked Fortune.

She took her limber Bible from the mantel in the big room. We gathered in a circle on the floor. One at a time, we closed our eyes and parted the Bible. We let a finger touch a verse which told us what the present was and what eternity would be.

If "it shall come to pass" or "it shall be" hid on the page, the Fortune was twice as strong. Mama, going on her fifth reading, knew which books of the Bible made things happen. And she interpreted the hardest ones for us. I got a string of "verily-verilies" and Mohab howling after Mohab.

When Jo fingered plagues and pestilence, she laughed and refingered for the coming of bridegrooms, for deer stags who could leap across green meadows.

Maudie never asked for seconds. While Jo read for her what her fingers found, Maudie's blue eyes rounded in wonder.

Once she got a verse that said that the bitter was sweet to the soul that hungered.

I thought it meant the wild flowers Maudie knew to eat—redbuds, sour grass, locust blooms—or the clay she let me help her nibble when nobody watched.

A better game was Wish Book. Each player repeated blind the Bible moves, but in a catalog. The reward was what the pointed finger cleared closest to. We had the three catalogs Sears Roebuck gave: Fall-Winter, Spring-Summer, and the smaller Christmas Special. We wore the pages wrinkled playing Wish Book.

Mama turned up harness, seeds, plowshares.

Jo fingered thin for frocks.

I got to play twice, for me and for Buck whose fingers were too curled for pointing. For myself, I knew the general location of the coloring books, of crayons with rainbows more than eight. For Buck my fingers found toys enough to fill three mail trucks.

Maudie's hands had not learned where the good things were. She usually got nails. Ax handles. Bedpans.

A tally was kept of prizes and their prices. At the end of five or ten, whatever times the players agreed on, the winner would be added.

Tractors and hardware brought bigger numbers, but everybody won. Then hands that had idled turned to hoes for the corn that Mama raised.

"Youens come see me," Maudie said.

"We will, an' you come," Mama said.

Maudie waited by the door for a piece of wheat bread on good days, cornbread on the average. Her blue eyes kept her bare feet company while she backed out the door.

Sometimes we watched her from the big room window. If Roland was in the fields, her path was never straight. She held Buck tight to her bosom while she parted barb wire to hand her gift away.

Daddy said they were hungry because Roland was to sorry to work in the mines. But Roland was scared of the dark.

Their land had been worn out before they came to it, and they could not afford fertilizer. In the spring and summer they made do, but in the best of years their potatoes never lasted beyond Christmas. Their corn never planted a second spring.

Maudie's rocky garden didn't yield right. And she had no jars to pickle summer in.

They had one skinny pig and some banty chickens that laid eggs no bigger than a thumbnail.

Roland wouldn't hire out. But when they needed winter food, he came unasked to chop our wood or mend our fences.

"The Lord will provide," he said to Daddy.

"Ye hear that, Lord?" Daddy said to Mama.

Mama gave double to get even for blasphemy.

In the early winter of my eighth year, Buck and Maudie came each weekday to play with me. I was sick with the lungs. Mama's daddy was even sicker. After I had thrown the fever, Mama went to care for him.

The mines had laid Daddy off. But he wouldn't sit in the

house. He counted trees all day or went to his brother Jaspar's to judge the bead on moonshine.

I boasted I could stay alone, but I was afraid of Raw Bones and Bloody Skull, of Haskew Fletcher who bit the nubs off little boys.

Before Jo left for school, Brownie announced Maudie carrying Buck, and the two skinny dogs and a sore-eyed cat following. Rags were tied around her feet. She had no shoes and she ran fast to beat frostbite. She wore an old Army coat and underneath the same dress as summer's.

Jo would point out the day's pintos already simmering on the stove, and a fritter left especially from breakfast.

As soon as Jo's song rounded the curve, Maudie got the fritter from the iron skillet. She nibbled while I measured Captain Midnight's tail or recounted the calendar's five Dionnes. She chewed some of the bread for Buck and hid the rest in her pocket.

Then I would bring out the catalog and we would move to the big room to play. We didn't keep tally. I didn't know double-line addition. But we pointed out and talked about our prizes.

"Pretty as a pup," Maudie said to my red wagon.

"Pretty as a pup," I said to her gray flannel.

"What on God's green earth is 'at?" she said to my crank Victrola.

"What on God's green earth is 'at?" I said to the bones of her corset.

We made up some new games. We counted how many times the same head peeped up from the necks of dresses, coats, robes.

"Red Head's twelve," I said from one Sears.

"Same's Raven Hair," she said from a second.

We searched to see if we could find somebody who didn't have a smile on. There were no children with sores, no sad women, though some men in mackinaws beaded mean into the sights of rifles.

I wondered why underwear had no heads or feet, just the middle.

"Mortify their faces if a Kodak caught 'em naked," Maudie said.

We exchanged Wish Books so I could feel all the crayons and she could touch all the baby clothes.

We chose and hunted our colors. Hers was blue. Mine the green and red of Christmas.

We liked to smell the slick pages, a crisp odor hinting of new linoleum.

Once she said to a full spread of apple trees, "Smells good nuff t'eat."

"Let's us try it," I said.

We tore the page from the catalog and divided it up three ways.

Buck spat his out. We laughed and almost choked, but I followed Maudie's swallow.

"Ever eat starch?" she asked.

I found Mama's Niagara, and Maudie and I pretended we were dipping snuff.

From last year's Wish Books we cut off the heads, past necks, of entire families and then headless outfits for every day and Sunday. When we put tops on bottoms, the heads were sometimes too small, sometimes too large, for the clothed bodies under the necks. A face with color might have a black-and-white trunk, but we weren't particular. We put them all through frets and fevers.

For a change, Maudie took down Mama's Bible and looked at the glossies. I knew them by heart and I told her about Joseph's coat of striped candy, of good Sammy and the beggarman, of Jesus going hunting for spring lambs.

She also liked to hear Mama's glow-in-the-dark signs that decorated the walls of all three rooms. I played I was reading them.

"Be Shore Yore Sins Will You Find Out."

"Ask an' You'll Get It."

"Knock an' Doors Will Open."

"John: 3.16."

"What's 'at mean?" she asked.

"Three dollars and sixteen cents," I said.

Maudie stopped all games at 10:30. We moved back to the kitchen where I nursed Buck and she mixed cornbread and peeled taters to go with the beans that needed more cooking than she could wait for. The taters she sliced into thin quarter moons. She added circles of onion. While the lard was frying one side, she sprinkled corn meal on top. She turned them once. They were white, moist, seasoned in their own iodine.

Roland brought to the table the scent of the sap of roots that his mattock had wakened.

At their house his voice could make muscles in the next room jerk, but he didn't talk in Mama's kitchen. He sat opposite me at the table. We tried not to eye each other.

Maudie sat by the cookstove and fed Buck.

As soon as Roland finished eating, he rose, silent, and went back to grubbing ground.

Maudie moved to the table. She used Roland's plate. She rolled the half-raw beans into cornbread, one at a time, and ate them fast.

"Hoover's little honger pills," she said.

If anything was left I divided it for Brownie and her dogs, for Captain Midnight and her cat. The Bible told Roland not to cast his bread unto dogs. Maudie liked to watch them eat.

"Swaller 'at thang," she said to whichever nosed the scraps in my palm. "Swaller 'at thang."

Maudie washed the dishes. I dried. Then we had three more hours to play.

If the blue veins of Buck's belly tightened him into sleep, I brought out my coloring book I got for being sick. Buck ate the crayons when he was awake.

Maudie and I lay down on the linoleum in front of the fireplace. She took one page, I the other.

Maudie laughed at all the animals dressed up like Christians. She could not color right. While I turned the yard of the Old Lady's shoe into a brag farm, she colored blue the gaping beak of Henny Penny. The face and lamb of her Little Bo Peep were purple. She couldn't even keep inside the lines. And she licked the crayons. But her eyes rounded blue and she laughed so hard I didn't have the heart to tell her what she was doing wrong.

When her teeth hurt she didn't laugh. She didn't play. She chewed tobacco and held the juice on the pain.

I chewed some too. It was bitter to the taste.

Once her pain was so hard she held Mama's iodine in her mouth, though cross-bones and a skull spelled out death.

I sinned when she cried. I turned Daddy's radio on. The batteries were for Roosevelt or Amos 'n Andy on a week night, for an hour of fiddles in the dark of Saturdays. Maudie was never around then. Roland didn't nightwalk, and Daddy didn't like strange ears eavesdropping in on his Philco anyhow.

I fingerprinted where the dials had been and turned them for Bessie up in heaven or hoecakes brown on earth. The music helped the pain go away.

"Can they hear us, ye reckon?" she asked.

Late November added Christmas to our Wish Book.

Maufie liked the pages of wavy chocolate candy, of oranges from afar, of fruit cakes that twinkled jewels. But when we made out our lists of presents — not in pencil, but in talk — she chose for Buck a jumpsuit with a hood as blue as his eyes. For Roland, a flashlight long as an arm. For herself, a pair of shoes that nurses wore. A sheepskin coat for my lungs.

I picked out ten colored frocks for her, the same ones as for Mama. Buck I gave a train that crossed two pages. A hope chest for Jo, and falsies and a cameo. My list was longer, for I also had Daddy, all of Mama's people, Daddy's.

She didn't have kin. And she wouldn't order Roland's people anything.

Before we could wish away all of December, Mama told her daddy to take up his bed and walk. He did. She came home to put her hand on my forehead and to rule that my lungs had dried.

I went back to school for my second year in the first grade, where the teacher let us trace pictures or help her make the hook rugs she sold for a bonus.

Mama didn't have time for games. She and Daddy hauled manure for the fields. Persuaded Nell the mare to yank boulders from the ground.

Maudie and Buck stayed home. But I had time with them. Everyday. The teacher let the low grades out early. I didn't wait for Jo. I built Maudie and me a collection of Wish Books so we could make longer our Christmas lists.

I knew which toilets had last year's catalogs. I slipped in and out of the Wamplers' for Montgomery Ward, the Comptons' for Aldens, the Perrys' for Spiegels, Fletchers' for Walter Fields, Nuckols' for National Bellas Hess.

I stole one a day until we had a full set. I put it in the belly of my overalls and held my hands in my front pockets to keep it in place. "Be shore yore sins will you find out" rang in my ears as I sneaked from the toilets and, once on the road, outran the posse from Revelation.

When I puffed steam through Maudie's door, she'd say, "Lordy-God-a-mighty, where'd ye git it at?"

"You go first," I said.

She closed her eyes and let her hands travel through new territory.

When we heard Jo argue with herself for Bub Colley's eyes, we put the Wish Book into a nest under the bed, and I went on home.

Christmas came too late. The company store cut Daddy off on the twenty-third.

But Jo and I got a candy bar in the toe of our stockings.

Maudie never said what she got.

She came rag-shod in the snow to watch us eat our Christmas. Daddy got mad and kicked the dogs off the porch on his way out to Jaspar's.

Maudie took her chair by the stove and pulled out a dry breast for Buck to butt on.

She gave no milk. Mama said that was why we had to make sure that Buck got something.

"Shore ye can't eat a bite?" Mama asked.

"Ain't a bit hongry," she said. She pushed back the strings of her hair and watched Buck practice his first teeth on her nipple.

"Give Buck some," Mama said.

Maudie put her breast back in her dress. She made Buck his wads of bread.

We played one game of Fortune from the New Testament, where Jesus lived.

Mama got shepherds. I got Herod. Jo got babies on the third try. Maudie found rocks and mountains falling on her.

Mama tied ribbons around three half-gallon jars of pickled beets and gave them to Maudie for a merry Christmas.

The next day I went down to her house to play. The skinny pig from its pen by the garden smiled red bruises at me. In the yard their last two banties pecked after a stray ball of wineness.

The dogs that usually slurped their dead ribbons between

their haunches now wagged them and smiled bleeding mouths for the palm of my hand. Even the cat had red whiskers.

Maudie's mouth and Buck's were ringed with the same red.

Three empty jars were on the table.

"We's had us a bait," she said. She rubbed her belly and laughed deep from her bosom, as if the vinegar had made her drunk.

We played one fast game of New Year's Wish Book, three prizes each, before we heard Roland bellow the dogs from his path.

Maudie held Buck tight to her breast and hummed a sound I didn't know.

I hid the catalog before Roland's feet found the steps.

I ran home.

The next day Maudie wouldn't play. Black circled her eyes and she had lost two teeth.

"Slipped on a patch a ice an' fell," she said.

I traced a train for Buck. He cried when I showed it.

The Dionne Quintuplets stretched their growth onto a new calendar. School started up again.

I brought my tracings home to show Maudie.

Her blue eyes looked at my Pocahontas bending her neck for the settler's ax, at my men in buckskin cupping hands over brows to help them see Kentucky. But her throat hummed the strange noise and her shoulders rocked wherever she sat.

The tails of the dogs weakened.

The cat forgot to purr when I scratched its ribs.

We ran out of corn.

Daddy sold the cow.

Roland started a rock fence around Mama's garden. It already had slats no chicken could crawl through.

Mama shook her head in wonder when she counted our empty jars.

Daddy cussed and went to Jaspar's.

Maudie dug deep into the frozen ground for Jerusalem artichokes.

She parted snow to look for buckberries.

Mama saved our tater peelings.

"Ask Maudie can she use these," she told me.

Maudie chewed them raw. She gave Buck pulp. It soured his stomach.

A false thaw came in early March. Maudie tied Buck to her back and climbed Cherry Mountain in search of greens.

A freeze took back the heady shoots of wild mustard, dock.

Her dogs licked Buck's used diapers.

The cat lifted a weak paw toward robins.

The pig hid in its cornshuck bed and refused the warm water she fed it.

Before it could die, Roland sold it and the two banties to his daddy.

$3.00.

He bought corn.

On my way to school I helped Maudie, barefoot and coatless, build a fire under her iron pot. She was going to bypass the mill, which took one-third, and turn the corn into hominy.

Mama lent her the lye.

That day I stole a live catalog from the Wamplers' mail box. It had an Easter woman on the cover, with daffodils, biddies, dyed eggs.

Maudie didn't thumb it once. She peered wildeyed into the pot and stirred the rising husks with the broken handle of a hoe.

"How long's it take?" I asked. I was hungry. We had cut out all mid-day food.

"Be soon," she said.

Her blue feet tapped out hoedown.

The dogs and cat waited on the road bank where they sniffed the steam that went uphill.

"Be good," she said.

Jo came to nudge me home before Maudie could start the nine rinsings.

"Youens come," she said. "Be plenty."

That night, after Roosevelt told us spring had come, we went to bed.

But not to sleep.

Roland came in the dark to get Mama to help Buck and Maudie die.

Daddy unbanked the fire. He turned the radio on.

Then he left to help Mama.

We sat silent till only static played.

Daylight drew Mama's face for us.

"Too late," she said. "She couldn't wait. She picked at the hominy before it was rinsed."

"Buck too," she said.

She hugged me and then passed the circle of her arms on to Jo.

Daddy stayed to help Roland bury the dogs who also hadn't waited. Then he went to find a casket on his credit.

Jo gave her blue nightgown she was saving for the bridegroom. She sent Buck her Shirley Temple comb. Mama gave my baby blanket she had hidden for a keepsake.

I had nothing to give, except my crayons and our Wish Books still hidden in their nest.

"Just you remember her like she was," Mama said.

That night she warned us, but I went with her to the wake.

The cat, with scabs for eyes, came out from under the porch to sniff my empty hands.

Maudie's table was heavy laden with sugar cakes, store bread, jars of peaches from some forgotten summer.

In the other room, women sang of heaven's open door and Preacher Singleton Bible drilled for Fortune and found a price that was above rubies.

Then the crowd parted enough for the forming of a line past the casket.

It wasn't Maudie. Nor Buck, cradled awkward on a stiff bent arm. The mouths were masked by gauze. The necks scarfed in bandages. Cheekbones blushed blue through rouge. Four nickels bought eyelids a costly sleep.

Mama petted the hands that lye had scaled. Then she stared straight into the humps of buffalo and cried for picnics in the sky.

I pushed through the growth that the tips of toes had given legs, unlocked the bones of mothers' hands that pulled their children's arms into the rigid gawk of May 1.

I ran to the cat's hiding place under the porch. I counted its ribs till purrs trembled the chill from my hands.

I didn't go back next day for the burying, but from the big room window I could hear them sing of blind wretches and grace that amazed them.

I got my picture tablet and lay down in front of the fireplace and tried to draw Maudie and Buck, without anything to trace them on.

I wasted paper. Their heads were white circles with blue lining the blanks.

I closed my eyes in daydream to dig up the way she laughed at the blue-beaked Henny Penny who cackled that the sky would surely fall. Her smile at the white bones of corsets. The lick of her finger as it chased a colony of cats that followed Dick Whittington around the curve of the next page.

At night real sleep took all the ruffles, all the lace. The popcorn eyes of banties flecked purple blood. Dogs grinned gums jeweled with maggots. The eyes of the cat dripped pus.

And Maudie, draped in chop-sack, lay heavy with her hunger. The head of Buck stretched for the perch of a shoulder blade. From under the gauze flowed the red wine of beets, its furrows following the blue ropes of veins that curved inward for the necks.

I waited for eye sockets to spit out their plugs to dance the blue of robin eggs that have been abandoned for the rain to cry on.

But the night could not afford the hue.

The Changing of the Guard

THE CHANGING OF THE GUARD

When his daddy emerged from the big room onto the porch, his eyes new-bandaged by mama and his dark glasses over the mask, Jess rose from the rocker he had wrestled from Hass and went to the kitchen mirror to wet down the flags of his hair. Hass jumped back into the chair and rode it just to set the rockers fanning. Then he followed. The three older brothers sat in silence round the table. Their eyes acknowledged Jess and one fewer hoe, now that he would be walking. Hass joined them. He squinted meanness at Jess and waved son-of-a-bitch by placing his right thumb on his nose and letting his four fingers flutter out the curse. Ben, the eldest, lifted a callused hand from cornbread crumbs and play-knuckled Hass on the head. "You'll get yore turn," he told Hass.

"His turn's been up a long time ago," Hass whined.

"But you ain't the talker he is," Ben said. Hass slammed the kitchen screen to go hide his pride behind the hollyhocks.

Ben rose from the table. " 'Is ain't buyin' the baby no shoes," he said. He didn't look at Doyle and Franklin who knew, anyhow, to pull themselves up for the dry cornfields that waited.

Jess' right hand met his daddy's left as the cane tapped out its patience on the porch floor. They crossed the front yard bare feet had worn down to clay and into the dirt road that would take them to the hardtop and half of the six miles to Nat's Store and Post Office.

They passed their lower fields, land his mama had brought to the union when her daddy died. Egbert stopped his cane to listen see could he hear the corn growing.

"How big's it, boy?"

"Waist high." Jess lied.

"Green?"

"Green's a snake's cud." The July drought had yellowed the corn, but Jess saw what it could have been. " 'Ey'll be three ears on ever stalk. Mock my word. Ever kernel'll be bigger'n a dime."

"Boy, I reckon you are the talker."

Jess looked straight ahead at the red gash of the road his bare feet could have mapped out blind. "Take atter my Uncle Martin."

"I pray not."

Uncle Martin was the only preacher in the family, but he didn't talk, not once the spirit or the liquor seized him. He screamed in an unknown tongue while his eyes pouched out and up toward heaven.

They were nearing The Pines, a wide place in the road flanked on both sides by thick spruce. It was a resting place for adults and fools, but Jess half-believed the tale that it was haunted and ran past it when he didn't have his daddy to guard. Hass always whimpered his way through. Raw Bones and Bloody Skull hid somewhere behind all that dark. He ate people alive, toenails to scalp.

"Don't glance to neither side. He's watchin' us, daddy."

"How's yore eyes turned?"

"I can see sideways. He's partin' pine to look see's we fat."

"All gristle an' bone," his daddy said, too loud.

"He might use us to practice on till Aunt Rhodie comes by." He hastened his daddy's feet into remembering when they could see. They aimed outward in long strides that dared rocks to get in their way.

They took their first rest at the Big Rock just beyond The Pines. Raw Bones didn't follow.

His daddy wheezed. "Boy, you'd better not let yore mama hear you talk 'bout her kin." Martin and Rhodie belonged to his mama.

"You said onct she should sell while the price a lard was high."

His daddy laughed he had.

Jess crawled to the top of the Big Rock while his daddy leaned against it. Jess aimed a fist at The Pines and preached, "Upon 'is rock I'll build my church." He tried a Martin scream, but his voice cracked on him.

His holler scared a raincrow from The Pines. "Daddy, look up!"

"What is it, boy?" His father's gauzed face aimed upward.

"Eagle. Big's a Piper Cub. Couldn't he care him off a child or two?"

"I reckon he could." Egbert removed his glasses and patted the bandages to see were they holding back the cancers.

"Ever seed a bigger one, daddy?"

"Can't says I have."

"At ole feller's bigger'n one you use't sang us." In olden times, his daddy had the patience to sing about an eagle that pecked out the eyes of a lost child.

"Looks just as hongry, too," his daddy warned.

"I'll shoo 'im off." Jess jumped from the rock and felt the clay bruise all fours. But he didn't rub flesh. He picked a round stone from the road and aimed it toward The Pines. The stone cut the hot air in flutters.

"Hit 'im?"

"'Ey's feathers fallin'."

"Guess he'll let us be."

"If he knows to tend 'is own business."

His daddy had regained his wind and they walked on through Ab Ray's apple trees that waved at both sides of the road. His daddy didn't know, but he and Hass stole apples there, ripe or not. Green ones made good war weapons. His family didn't have an orchard. Took all their land for corn.

"How's the Wine-Sap doin'?"

"Looks like the tree blight passed it by. Big. Tree limbs almost brushin' the ground." Its trunk was half-eaten by wood ants, and only a few knotted apples clung to its gnarled limbs.

"Was a sight when I was a boy."

"Still holds its purpose."

Next was the Johnson pasture with the black cows Jess hated. Two of them had gotten into their corn that spring and had made replanting necessary. He and Hass had sicked the dogs to eat their tails and scare them into dryness.

"Ole Johnson's pasture," Jess mumbled.

"How's his herd?"

"Scrawny. Got dirt moustaches from eatin' crab-grass roots." Johnson had threatened to sue, but settled on five bushels of last year's corn when his milk cows got back their flow and grew new hair on their tails.

" 'At's a shame."

It would not have been a shame if they were fly-blown instead of fleshy, but his daddy wouldn't blaspheme anything.

"We got to look out for 'em Johnsons. 'Ey'll probably rock us when we pass 'eir barn."

"'Ey won't lay a hand on us, boy."

"Might not on you. You got glasses on, an' 'at's against the law."

The Johnsons were resting on their porch swing and rockers, but he talked loud so his daddy couldn't hear their squeaks and throw up his cane to answer hello to their hands. Even his mama hadn't spoken to the Johnsons since they threatened to sue.

"Slow down, boy. I can't high-tail like you." His daddy stopped to take a cancer pill without water to chase it down.

"We's almost to the river."

"River can wait."

And it did. For them to sit in Jess' favorite place under the covered bridge, to listen to the gurgle and watch the fish, though what fish was left in the almost dry river had found rocks to hide under.

Jess took the makings for a cigarette from the bib pocket of his daddy's overalls and rolled Egbert a rest. He took two deep draws before placing it in his daddy's moisting mouth. The smoke made Jess' head swim.

Jess put his feet in the water to clean them for the walk on the State Highway. His daddy had taught him that, to be clean and presentable.

"Wont to cool 'em feet?" Jess asked.

"Don't care if I do," his daddy answered. They shared the pulling off of a shoe and sock, and then he guided his father's feet into a small pond rocks had kept full.

"Feet sloshed up any fish?" Jess asked.

"Can't says 'ey have."

"I stepped on a big one," Jess' feet lied.

"What kind was he?"

"Ain't never seed one like 'im. Green scales an' purple eyes."

"Never seed one like 'at."

"A stranger to these parts. 'At much I'll say."

Jess gathered some broad dock leaves to dry his daddy's feet. He let his own drip on the hot white rocks. Then he helped to tie his daddy's shoes.

"Reckon I'm old enough for summer shoes?" Jess asked, as his fingers tightened a bow. His daddy's silence didn't take the hint.

"Ready to step on, daddy?"

"Ready's I'll ever be."

They climbed the bank and crossed the bridge to the big road where Jess guarded his daddy from the cars that would run a normal man over if he didn't have 20-20 and a fast broad jump.

"Traffic's worsenin' up," his daddy noticed.

"Miners' vacation. Be a heap dead come Monday."

"Tell me the cars as 'ey pass."

And Jess told off the names he had heard at school. He knew a Ford from a Chevrolet, but the others looked alike. "Pontiac, Packard, LaSalle, Studebaker, Cadillac, Willis. Two Hudsons in a row." He also knew all of the nations and many of the tribes of American Indians.

"No Fords?"

" 'Ey too rich now't drive Fords," he said.

A Ford truck whooshed by. Its wheels caught the middle of a snake and pasted it in its own juices to the hard-top.

"Daddy. A snake." He nudged his father into the ditch while his tongue told its breed. "A rattler." A garter snake squirmed both ends of its bruised body. The tar held on.

"Be careful, boy. It's Dog Days."

"It's gone be dead days for one long rope of a rattler." His hands chose a rock that the hillside wouldn't give. He settled on a smaller one.

"Don't ye get too close. An' don't let 'im see yore teeth." His daddy didn't need to tell him. He knew teeth would rot out if a snake saw them in Dog Days.

Tight-lipped, he dropped the stone on the orange ring below the snake's head. Only the tail now twitched. It would tremble, he knew, till the sun went down.

"Smashed 'is head, daddy."

"You sure he's out?"

"A goner." He let his father's cane feel the tremble the tail gave. It felt like fishing.

"Any rattlers?"

"Ten, best I can see."

"Cut 'em off. Give the boys back home a show."

"I ain't about to whittle 'at tail." He pushed inward, almost toppling his daddy, to duck an unbathed miner in a Chevrolet.

"Sassy black man in a Studebaker."

"You reckon?" His father had never seen a black man. Jess had seen some in the Congo of a geography book.

"Better not let the sun set on 'is back."

"I reckon he's got a right to travel."

"Not when he smatters folks on 'is windshield."

They rounded Sickle Curve, and Jess stopped to point out again the cliff that had claimed so many in car wrecks. He kept a tally on Sickle Curve, thirteen souls and one child that hadn't reached accountability. The stains had long since dried, but with his father's cane he tapped out where they had been. " 'Is newest one's Rob Horton."

His father's cane jerked it didn't want to hear the stains.

They passed a mangy hound, and Jess started to call him a mad dog; but he could see his daddy didn't need the talk. Jess counted the candy wrappers and beer cans in the inward ditch. The beer cans were ahead when the Mail Truck braked to ask did they want a lift to Nat's.

Their slow pace had made the ride necessary. Jess preferred walking all the way. His tongue tied on him when it had to allow others their say.

Nory Hess was in the cab. He fumbled with his daddy toward the covered truck bed.

" 'Ey's plenty room for ye up here, Egbert," Junior Tiller yelled backward.

"We thank ye," his daddy said for both of them. Jess led him to the opened door and showed his feet the running board.

He sat on his daddy's lap. His hair brushed the windshield.

"Which one yore boys is 'at?" Junior asked. He didn't look at Jess or his daddy. His eyes aimed the gear stick up and then down to spread Nory's dress tail.

"Next to the last," his daddy said.

Junior Tiller had raked Jess' face for the four years he had been his daddy's guard, but he always had to be retold.

"How many's it make?"

"Fourth, but he's seed me through the most." Ben, then Doyle and Franklin, had led his daddy when he was just blind. Jess' time had come with the cancers.

Their words turned to the weather. Jess was glad to be left to his reflection in the windshield.

"A scorcher," Junior allowed.

"Have seed hotter," his daddy offered.

"I can stand up to the day heat." Nory squirmed. "Hot nights is what gets me down," she said.

Jess' side vision saw Junior's lips dog a grin and his gear hand gain on Nory's legs. He knew Junior picked folks up so Nory would have to scrunch to him. Nory rode any vehicle that bothered to brake for her.

"Like take me a ride to catch a day breeze to think about while I flail the sheets a night." She looked at Junior and laughed her out some air.

His daddy shifted Jess' weight to his left knee, and Jess' face turned to see Nory's hand pretend a second gear shift in Junior's lap.

Junior changed gears when there was no rise. Jess felt his face juice red. He stuck his head out the window to air out his shame.

His daddy's words sought out Nory's husband, her babies. Junior's mama. Their husky voices allowed their health as the truck slowed to a crawl his feet could have passed. He looked at the limestone the road was chopped from and tried to see it as the Grand Canyon in geography.

The truck crunched gravel and Jess had his door open before Junior and Nory could unruffle. He positioned his daddy safe by Nat's screen door and stood by to pay for their ride by relieving Junior of the gray bags of mail. He saw Nory shift to the right side of the cab to wait for gears to guide her to the next post office.

Junior climbed into the truck bed. There in the shade he cupped his groin and gave it a flick-flick-flick, the way Jess' daddy judged the ripeness of a melon. He winked at Jess to plant on his brow a hot secret. Jess bowed his head to acknowledge the branding.

Junior dismounted, and before Jess could lug inside the two gray bags, Junior's hand opened on a quarter new as dawn. "Buy yeself somethin' sweet to chew on," Junior whispered. Jess' right hand dropped its burden to strike at the silver.

Junior promenaded first into the store. "I'm here with what everybody's been waitin' for," he announced.

"Not onless you's the Lord God a Hosts," somebody in the store said.

"Amen, Brother Viers," other voices agreed.

Junior didn't stay long enough to say what he was.

The store was full of baptizers from Salt Creek who were praising the Lord and pulling puckers out of their wet clothes. Jess directed his daddy to an empty powder keg on the store side. He stood across by the closed post office window to wait see did they get any mail. They never did, except relief on the first, to compensate for blindness. But he and his daddy liked to look for a surprise.

The baptizers kept Nat busy crossing from the post office to the store side to collect for their sardines and candy, with pop to chase them down. Jess wanted to buy him and his daddy a cool drink, but he knew he'd have to tell how the coin came to its hot nest in his pocket.

He recognized most of the crowd by face, some of them by name, but he was glad their tongues were too busy with miracles wrought to acknowledge him. He listened to a woman who had always choked on solid food and who now ate peanut brittle. He heard of a blind boy who had never seen daylight, then saw his kin. Others under affliction had received the touch of Brother Viers' right hand and had quickened into victory. The service was picking up again, and Nat was too rushed to inform them they weren't at church.

"Lay ye hand on Brother Egbert," Jess heard someone say. Refired by their snacks, the baptizers gathered around his daddy and started to pray.

"The blind shall see," Brother Viers declared. He pulled a Bible from his armpit and started shuffling the leaves to find a verse to prove he was right. He knelt by Egbert's powder keg before he found it. Others followed suit.

In the hush of mumbles, the flies that swarmed the candy seemed larger than bats. The preacher's Bible thickened into the rock that God had burnt his ABC's on.

Someone whispered to him, "Ye wont ye pore daddy to see, to lead ye home, now don't ye boy?" Brother Viers' hands were pressing hard at both sides of his daddy's head. Jess closed his eyes and nodded yes with his neck. The rest of him was frozen.

Brother Viers dropped his hands, and the whispers lowered. The store crowd divided up sides and gave Jess a dead aim on miracle. He blinked out the light, but his ears thought they were eyes and saw Lazarus licked and loaves of light bread sliced for smiling sardines. A sea of grape pop parted and the souls of Sickle rose to dance their way to weddings. He prized his eyelids open.

Brother Viers was ready to see had the cure taken. Mama always did the service at home. Daddy wouldn't let anybody else, except the hospital, see the unveiling.

Egbert's hands fought off bees that weren't there. Brother Viers whispered them quiet.

Nat opened the window, but no one shifted tracks for mail.

First came the glasses. The tape. Then the thin layers of gauze, delicate as the wings of moths. One by one Brother Viers scaled them off. The red and yellow stains grew from dots to eggs. The hands brought the last pad from the eyes and nose. A bright bone hooked through flesh and two orange eyes pushed at thin red ropes. The air caught the open sores that dripped their tears in pus for the other rounded eyes to see. The preacher's hands brushed the sockets, tampered with their unripe cores.

Jess heard the cartilage of his throat swallow curds of puke. His tongue moved, but the words were trapped in the cave of his mouth. He saw his daddy's neck and shoulders cry.

His feet found their courage and walked to his daddy. Hands came from their caverns to help. The shiny quarter fanned and found the preacher's opened palm. Jess helped the gauze cover his father's nakedness.

"Maybe tomar, when he rises?" Brother Viers whispered.

The crowd parted to let them pass.

They walked in silence, past Sickle, its curve no more than a gentle arm cradling them to limestone. They passed the garter snake wreathed in sunset round its stone. The river didn't gurgle, but a raincrow promised rain. The black cows nestled in a knot around a tree. Jess threw up his free hand to the Johnson boys and their dog who were separating dry from wet.

They rested under The Pines. His daddy took a pill while Jess gazed up through the dark limbs to find the fluff of clouds.

"Time you had summer shoes," his father said.

"My feet can take it."

"Time too we changed the guard."

"I'll miss the sights we've seed."

The white mask caught his eyes and pulled them down. "Son, you've seed all 'ey is to see."

"Yes, sir." His hand caught his father's to help it squeeze a grip on the cane.

"I'll see 'at Hass knows 'is turn's come," Jess said.

Though his eyes couldn't see through their scalding rain, Jess felt his cane regain their rhythm of walk.

The Father

THE FATHER

Mrs. Percy C. Breeding turned right off dirt and onto hardtop without looking for other cars, so relieved she was that her motor still ran, her tires were still full. As School Board Officer and Welfare Caseworker, she had in her time suffered many flats. Sugar in the gas line. Clay up her exhaust. More dents than she could shake a stick at.

Her worst had happened in the very holler she was leaving, when she came to tell Trilla Lambert that the State would not pay for her last woodscolt, and to try to chase the two of attendance age back to the Copperhead grade school. They draped a cow afterbirth across Mrs. Breeding's radiator. She sickened on the fry until her husband Percy Calvin, "Doc Rabbit" to trash, looked under the hood to find what slime was left.

"I truly believe I could give more to the County, the State, and the Nation if I did not have to serve two masters," she said to her imaginary Supervisor, a little blue-haired lady who sometimes rode with her. On bad days the Head Man shared the front seat. She could never make out all of his features, but she knew she shared eye-to-eye with him.

"The father calls many," the Supervisor said. "He chooses few."

Mrs. Percy C. Breeding yawned at the wisdom. She had two more stops, both, she thanked her God aloud, just off the State Highway.

The first was to make sure that all the idiots in Finis Presley's house had suffered through six more months of life.

"Such obstinate cases," she said to her Supervisor, though she really didn't mind the Presleys when they were not sporting fevers. Idiots always smiled up at her, even when she was removing them from the roll.

"If the State just knew half the pity of it," the Supervisor said, once Mrs. Breeding cleared her throat for the high whine.

"And I do right by them all," said Mrs. Breeding, an octave lower. "Unless they bring me grief and disappointment."

"Seven times seven," said the Supervisor, who sometimes talked jibberish.

Mrs. Breeding lucked out on the first stop. Finis Presley was walking, almost running, on her side of the road. She pulled up beside him. Waved his hand from the chrome handle and yelled through glass, " 'Ey all 'live? Ye sisses an' ye bruver?" She had to talk hick. Trash did not understand English.

"Sick," he said. He held up three fingers for them all. "Awful bad. Ride to town. Doctor."

She supposed he hadn't heard that Dr. Sullivan no longer traveled. She rolled down the window enough to poke out her clipboard and a pencil. "Just mark ye X 'ere on 'at last line," she said.

His hand trembled out the letters of his full name.

She took back her clipboard and pencil. "See youens in six months," she said and left him, his fingers still curling for the pencil and his one eye wild in what looked to be a coming storm.

She turned the wipers on to fight the peppered rain.

"His family's even more pitiful," she said to the Supervisor. Syphilis, incest, and stupidity, she would have told the Head Man. She forced herself to sneeze possible germs into her glove before she built up speed.

"*Our* family," said the Supervisor.

Mrs. Breeding wanted to say she knew her kin — all dead — and that if others had recognized their own cousins, God's green earth might not be cluttered with vermin. But she swallowed her frustrations and hummed "Father's Over Yonder."

"Well, you do work wonders," the Supervisor said. "You discover their level and utilize it."

Mrs. Breeding could have said she learned their ways from her husband, who had hovered around trash before she married him. Wore silly clothes and staggered from wine. Instead, she counted her wonders. Orvil Compton, sent off to Blind School, could now multiply in his head. Harris Deel, from a family of dimwits, worked the night shift in a rubber plant in Ohio.

"I do my very best," Mrs. Breeding said.

"Your brother's keeper," the Supervisor said and bowed her head.

"Two sets of tires a year," Mrs. Breeding said.

The next stop was to be Nanny Spradlin's to add on for her sixth bastard. Mrs. Breeding had intended to stop yesterday but Ferrel Ringstaff's Ford, all decorated with the tails of dead animals, had been parked below the two-room shack. She had not felt up to that whorehop, come with the pretext of seeing Nanny dance the Charleston she claimed she learned in Hollywood.

Her gloves tightened in on the wheel. The road ahead seemed to be a spool of film unwinding and she, not Nanny Spradlin, was in it—a newsreel with cannons and trumpets and drums. She walked rigidly into a huge arena. She wielded a butcher knife and whacked off dicks, past gristle, on a long line of obedient whore hops and morons. Above, in a special booth, the Head Man applauded. Flag poles shook for him and for her.

For years she had wished the State would go back to castrations and hysterectomies. Except she would add trash to their old list of criminals and crazies. Plus the stupid who didn't know to stretch rubbers over dicks.

She forgot the Head Man wasn't there and said, "Burn out all the tumors."

The Supervisor thought she was talking of wens.

Mrs. Breeding closed her out. Heard instead bulldozers pushing bodies into a gaping ditch.

"The Father up in heaven," the Supervisor said. "He knows our every thought."

Mrs. Breeding stopped on a dime. "Out," she said.

The Supervisor obeyed without words.

In privacy, Mrs. Breeding threatened an orphan home for Nanny's children.

The sow shifted her eyes and hugged whichever children she could reach without getting out of her rocker. More pracious'n jewels, she claimed. More pracious'n gold.

"I hear we are reviving the KKK," Mrs. Breeding said to her now—and had actually said earlier, much to her own pain and embarrassment, for the hussy had written Washington and two FBI's came to question loafers at Nat's Store and Post Office about the life and habits of Miss Pineford Kiser. When they told them she had been Mrs. Percy Breeding for years, they wanted to know his politics and how much wine he drank.

"You rip-whore-slut-bitch-trollop," she spat out, her face so flushed she had to turn the heater down.

On her glance upward she caught the Head Man's wink, between swathes of the windshield wipers.

He was sliding into the front seat with her. She could tell by the crinkle of electricity building up for a spread. "These bleeding hearts," she said. "Since Roosevelt."

"If we could just burn out the trash," she said. "Then start all over." Sometimes they saw a land where men took account of their sperm. Where women knew when to keep their legs crossed.

His eyes pierced straight ahead for the future. And the slight rise of his chin and a quick wink told her she'd march with him.

"You are mortifying me to the very bone," she said.

She passed Nanny's before she realized she was there. She had to back up to the wide place by the footpath that led up to the shack.

She invited the Head Man to go with her, but she knew he would not deign to suffer such fools.

From the glove compartment she took a twelve-gross box of condoms the State intended for all of Copperhead but which she meant for Nancy Spradlin. She put it into the gape of the purse some children called a granny bag. She threw her companion a quick kiss and followed the sound of "White Christmas" on the radio.

She hipped her free hand and rested in the yard of tin cans, rocks and one dead cedar, its brown limbs and needles trembling in the wind. Under a floor post hovered two skinny cats and an almost hairless dog gnawing on the therapeutic ball the State had given Nanny's eldest to help it get over polio.

She knocked on the first door, the kitchen, without removing her gloves.

She heard the slap of bare feet on linoleum. A squeak. A cry. Then the radio lost its sleighbells in the snow for a child to question: "What is it an' what ye wont?"

"I am here to investigate the birth of the child. Its father. Nor do I have until Doomsday."

Feet thumped and slapped as if she had said she was from some cave.

"Ol' Welfare Woman," she heard through the wood.

"Ol' School Depaty."

"Ouuuuu," they shivered out.

"I do not have a warrant," Mrs. Breeding said. School was out till after New Year's.

" 'At's Miz Kizer" came from a husky voice in the second room. "Let 'er in, er she'll care ye off in 'at big ole satchel."

"Mrs.," she snapped, "and Breeding," just as the door opened on the smell of onions and sores.

A child's head, shaved against lice, peeped out to grunt a greeting.

Mrs. Breeding held a gag behind a gloved hand.

Slops were trying to sour in a bucket by the cookstove. A dish-pan of soiled diapers rested on the table.

The cripple the County had tried to help led her through the kitchen and into the other room where a potbellied stove gave out a ring of heat not large enough to dry the snot that slipped from the noses of four other children crowding Nanny and the baby in the chair.

"Clean off side a my bed for Miz Kiser," Nanny said.

The crippled girl spread a mildewed quilt over sheets that had never seen soap or water. She stepped back for the guest to sit.

"I'll just stand by the window," Mrs. Breeding said. She didn't talk hick around Nanny who supposedly had "been places."

"Give 'er 'at powder kag, youngen," Nanny said.

The second tallest, bald like the rest, scooted a mining keg within the reach of Mrs. Breeding who put it between the two beds. She pulled aside the curtain, a piece of moldy oilcloth nailed to the window, to give herself light.

"Get us some bubs when a check comes in," Nanny apologized to the bulbless cord that hung from the ceiling.

Mrs. Breeding sat. She glanced up at the movie stars and calendars of Jesus that circled the walls of the room.

The cripple fiddled with the knobs on the radio.

"Leave hit off," Nanny said. "Company."

In the weak light and through Nanny's cigarette smoke, Mrs. Breeding could see that delivery had not changed the mousey hair thinned from too many home permanents. The breasts no harness could contain. Churns of legs crawling in long black hairs.

And men came from three counties to watch her tiny feet hold up all that quiver. Children even played hooky to hear her tell of Hollywood.

Through the leather of her gloves, Mrs. Breeding felt her pen. "Miss Spradlin," she started. "That is still your name, is it not?" She had gone by Pair-Power-Crosby.

"Paddlin' Spradlin," one of the children said.

"Mr. Cetificate," Nanny said. "Hit don't lie."

"This visit will serve, too, as your bi-annual review," Mrs. Breeding said. All she really needed was the father of the new bastard, but she always tried to trick Nanny into fraud.

"Go ahead, shoot," Nanny said.

The smallest walking child pointed a finger at Mrs. Breeding and said, "Pow-pow-bang-bang."

"You little scutter," Nanny said and swiped at air with her free hand.

"Starting with the first, I need the name and address of the father," Mrs. Breeding said.

"Same's allis, 'cept for Ash Lee," Nanny said. She flapped one side of the baby's blanket for Mrs. Breeding, who did not rise.

"Less see," said one child.

"Less see," said another.

All five crowded around to look down upon him.

"I do not have till Doomsday," Mrs. Breeding reminded.

"Hurry, youngens. Line up now," Nanny commanded. "Miz Kiser's in a big hurry."

They made a semi-circle around the far half of the stove, so that they were facing Mrs. Breeding.

"Little Darnell," Nanny said for the oldest. "My first born." The child's small head favored its mother's, but her skin was so white the blue veins could be seen pumping in her neck. Her left arm dangled from polio, the palm of its hand cupped outward.

Mrs. Breeding pretended to write on a form.

"By Tyrone Pair, when I'z in Hollywood, hired girl for the Stars."

The first time Mrs. Breeding had called, Nanny had pulled out trashy clothes from an old trunk. Named each item from a star: Betty Grable for a corset, Rita Hayworth for a skirt. And on past quit-time.

"Now, Miss Spradlin, are you sure of the child's father?" The forms read Tyrone for the County, unknown for the State and the Nation. Mrs. Breeding had more sense than to risk their inspection with half of Hollywood.

"Had to be," Nanny said and rolled her beady black eyes. She held Ash Lee close to count nine of her fingers. "Didn't see no other daddy. Didn't much wont to."

"Have you heard from the father in the past six months?" Mrs. Breeding asked.

"Lord, we ain't even seed a pitcher show," Little Darnell said.

At the beginning, when their Welfare was Relief, Mrs. Breeding had threatened to cut them off if they kept riding the mail truck to the county seat and the movies.

"Miss Spradlin, have you been in touch, in any form or fashion, with the child's father?"

"Ain't seed hide ner hair," Nanny said. "A marrit man, anyhow, but marrit in Hollywood...."

Mrs. Breeding did not want to get her started. "Next," she said.

"Dixie Lee," Nanny said for the second girl, a mess of freckles and dirt squatting by the coal bucket to get ducks on Nanny's cigarette. She bore no resemblance to the first or to Nanny.

"Clark Grable," Nanny said.

"Gable," the child corrected and pointed to his picture above Nanny's bed.

Little Darnell bent to rake some soot onto her good pointing finger. Dixie Lee put her tongue under her upper lip for the drawing of a little moustache.

"Looks just like 'im," Nanny said.

"Ol' Hitler," said Little Darnell.

"Less see," said two at once.

"Daddy ain't got in touch since she's a baby," Nanny said. She dropped her cigarette into the bucket.

Dixie Lee picked it out of coal. She rocked on her haunches as she drew smoke in through blackened teeth, let it out through her nose.

The next one, Carole L., was the fattest in what could have been a ward for rickets. She sashayed to the pout of her lower lip.

"Bang Crosby," Nanny said. "Was when I warshed dishes for 'is wife."

Mrs. Breeding doodled around the previous claims that Crosby was the father of Dixie Lee, Gable the father of Carole. Yet the County would not accept the shift as fraud.

"Ain't talked to 'im, 'ceptin' on the radio," Nanny shot the gun to say. "He's tight anyhow. Blood in a turnip."

The children stared in disbelief that anyone who gave "White Christmas" could be a skin-flint.

"Yessireemam," Nanny said. "Tight's ye can hear 'im squeak."

"The twins," Mrs. Breeding said.

"Claudette C. an' Lana T.," Nanny said. " 'Ey belongt' Dick Power an' John Garfield."

They did look as if they came from separate fathers. Claudette C. played with the scabs on her head and then looked down to her feet which took after her mama's. Lana T. had a few tufts of jet hair. Her feet were big enough to hold years of growth, if it ever came.

Lana T. belonged to Ferrell Ringstaff, as anyone who had peeped his swimmy eyes could have told.

Mrs. Breeding said his name.

"Nosireemam," Nanny said.

"Place of birth?"

Nanny pointed to the bed Darnell had covered. "Right der," she said. "After'n I excaped Hollywood."

"I recollect ever last step," said Little Darnell, who claimed she could draw all of California if she had the crayons.

Mrs. Breeding nodded toward the baby under the blanket.

Nanny spread both flaps and showed a little redhead with slits for eyes and mouth and a button of a nose already trained to dribble snot. With her right hand, she guided out of her dirty bodice a three-ringed gland. She raised the baby's mouth to the nipple. It sucked as if its very life depended.

The children gathered around to help Nanny grin at the rooting.

"Father?" asked Mrs. Breeding. She expected the latest star they had heard on the radio.

"Ondly one with a Copperhead daddy," Nanny said.

Mrs. Breeding aimed her pen at the line of parentage. "Ferrell Ringstaff," she said and started to write.

"Nosireemam," Nanny said.

Mrs. Breeding waited for Pop Man, Bread Man, or Mail.

"Ol' Doc Bunny," Nanny said and winked into air.

"Wabbit," corrected one twin.

"Wabbit-wabbit," said the other.

The pen pushed through paper.

"Come to see me ever day Ferrell's up in Dayton," Nanny said.

"Percy Calvin Breeding has never set foot in this sty," Mrs. Breeding said.

Nanny's eyes crossed, and the children looked puzzled.

"Ol' Doc's all I know," Nanny said. "Come to see me dancet."

"What's up Doc?" Little Darnell said in imitation of the rabbit on one of Percy's trashy caps.

"Brung us candy eggs," said Dixie Lee.

"An' Virginnie Dare wine," said Nanny.

Mrs. Breeding coughed to restart her heart. Before she broke Percy, it had been Virginia Dare. But anyone at Nat's could have told.

The baby whimpered until he got back his titty.

Mrs. Breeding could have sworn she heard blow-flies, and in December.

A child started humming "The Old Gray Goose is Dead," the song Percy used to slobber out when he drank heavy and had to puke in the coal bucket.

Mrs. Breeding saw mortification type itself out in triplicates and quadruplets all the way to Washington. In a hand impeded by its glove and her tremble, she wrote unknown in the blank. She didn't bother with midwife, eye drops, shots — all the absurdities the State and Nation now demanded. She humped up courage and tried to rise.

"Asleep," she whispered, when she staggered. "Foot's asleep."

"Youngens, two ye latch on to 'er," Nanny said. "Pore thang's gone faint."

She pushed them away with her purse. The box fell out.

She let hands raise it toward her. She motioned it on to Nanny.

"Better use these," she whimpered into the smoking face.

The children tore the box open and pulled out rubbers for all.

"Money," said one, for the foil around them.

"Bal-loons," said another.

Mrs. Breeding swirled away from the shaved heads, the rounded mouths.

On her fast way down the path, she fell and got red mud on her navy blue.

She couldn't remember finding her keys, unlocking the car. She even forgot that the Head Man might still be there. She talked to Percy instead. Called him whorehop and stuttered for other words that might hold his sorriness. "Thought disease'd dried the lust from yore loins," she said. "An' now ye gone an' ruint my Christmas. The one time I can sit back an' hum somethin' close to happiness."

When she repeated the words to his face, he squirmed in his easy-chair and denied he was the father. Said he didn't even know Nanny.

Three years before, come April, he had told her of the tiny feet in Charleston.

"Was from Nat's," he said and gave his face free twitch. "Never laid eyes on 'er. Never set foot in 'er house." He held the heart the doctors called a miracle. "Where eggactly did ye say she lived?"

She refused to sit at the table with him.

She would not share their featherbed. She wouldn't even remind him to take the five medicines that kept him going.

She invited the Head Man to share her couch-bed, but he would not come inside.

All night long the parts of the bastard baby mixed with Percy's legs, thighs, even the belly that pouched a navel outward. And a circle of little girls hissed, "Less see, less see."

The next morning, while he sipped weak coffee at the table, she stood over him and laid down the laws:

His car would be sold. He would not need one in his life to come.

He would never again leave her sight, except to feed her shepherd Blondie or spit tobacco off the porch. She never had let him chew in the house.

He would ride with her. If he was unable to climb the steps to some house of contagion or crime, he was to sit stone-still in the car. She dared him to so much as roll down the window.

"Kill me," he whimpered.

"Take it or leave it," she said.

He took it because he knew he couldn't pay for the chemicals that went down his gullet to keep him alive.

She hurried him into his going clothes for her last workday before Christmas. She marched him to her car. She opened the passenger door for him. Locked him inside.

Once the car had warmed up, he turned the radio on.

She cut it off.

He looked straight ahead into sun on new snow.

She got a glimpse of the Head Man through the windshield, but he couldn't enter, not with another man in his seat.

Percy's fingers played music on the dashboard.

"Hush!" she said.

Below Nanny's, she slowed to a crawl. She glared at him to see if he would look uphill.

Morning into noon, she worked the graveled roads of Greasy Creek. Visited three sorry families whose children came out into the cold to wave at Percy in the car.

On her way back, she stopped at Nat's to mail some forms. "Stay put," she told Percy.

Her entrance disrupted the talk of a circle of men.

She heard Nanny's name, a Christmas tree, Ole Doc Rabbit.

"Did someone refer to my invalid husband?" she asked.

Nat rose from his rocker and blushed his way to the Post Office side.

The other men pretended they had to spit into buckets.

She mailed her letter and got back into the car just as Percy was trying to squirm out.

"Stay put," she commanded. "We gone go see ye woman." The store already knew. She might as well do what she had considered last night—drag him up to their very bed of fornication. Rub his nose in the cat shit under it.

His breathing sounded like the death rattles she saw her daddy through.

"Ain't gone go," he said. "Can't make me."

She threw her head back and gurgled out a laugh which she turned into a hum that lasted all the way to the wide place below Nanny's.

She heard whoops and giggles but she could not see their source from her side of the car.

Percy's head was aimed uphill, though, and she could read terror in his eyes.

"Out," she said.

He would not budge.

The bright sun blinded her. She had to hold onto the car to walk around to his side.

She guessed the key into the lock, but his finger held down the little knob.

She left the key in and shielded her eyes to look uphill.

Barefoot children were dancing in snow around the dead cedar that had blossomed overnight. Inflated and tied condoms flapped in circles around it. Others bulged under the branches to give the tree a new belly. On top, for its star, hung what Mr. Percy Calvin Breeding had called his go-to-hell-cap, aimed toward the road, its bill crowned by a rabbit saying WHAT'S UP DOC?

Children called down, "Mur Christmas, Miz Kiser." Some started down the path to meet her.

They recognized Percy before they got to the bottom. "Mommie," they yelled back, "Ol' Welfare Woman's found Ash Lee's daddy."

Doc Rabbit lowered his head into cupped hands.

The children surrounded her. Fingerprinted her chrome and laughed into the window at their latest daddy and called, "Candy," and, "Christmas gift."

From the kitchen door came Nanny's husky voice: "Wait fer me, youngens. Wait for ye bruver, now."

The children pulled at Mrs. Breeding's navy blue. "Come looky't our tree," they begged. "Come go see Christmas."

Nanny was easing her way down the hill, her feet slowed by the weight of the baby.

Mrs. Breeding tried to shoo the children off with her loose glove.

Then she caught Doc by surprise. She yanked the door wide open.

"Out," she said. She pulled him into rise and out of the car.

He slumped to the ground. Tried to hug her back tire.

She jerked her spine rigid. She slapped away the bones of children's arms to squeeze back into her car.

The horn cleared the road.

She burnt rubber to get away.

Around every curve she looked for the Head Man, but he wasn't there.

In the yard, Blondie leapt and whined for Doc.

"Gone," she said. "Gone forever."

Though darkness had not closed in, Miss Peneford Kiser donned her one lacy nightgown. She went on to her featherbed. Once she was warm enough to squirm around, she pulled a sheet tight through her fork. Her thighs squeezed in to the sting.

A window opened. Or was it the door?

She smiled and waited.

His boots dropped to the side of the bed. His uniform rustled. The miracle was that, through closed eyes, she could see all of him for the very first time. He was shorter, whiter than she had thought. But he glittered. Glowed.

She played shy until he inched himself against her. Then she whispered that he was her baby, her little man, and her fingers slicked his black hair to the left of his forehead.

He hacked his chin into her shoulderblade. She pulled his head up and took into her mouth the square moustache no wider than his nostrils, flared.

"A thousand years," her voice husked as he started helping her to build up to her slow burn.

Idie Red, Idie Blue

IDIE RED, IDIE BLUE

Two peas in a pod, everybody said. But Gaye knew different. They didn't even have the same birthstone. Faye was born at 11:46 p.m., June 20, 1935. Five and one-half pounds. Red stone. Gaye followed at 12:01, June 21. Under five pounds. Green stone.

Mama Maye didn't give enough milk. Faye got titty. Gaye got Ole Sookie in a bottle. Faye slept through thunder. Gaye was fitful and wet the bed.

Faye was the first to crawl, to walk, first to bleed, first to be born again, first under at the baptizing.

And when they found out God had given them singing, Faye sang lead. Gaye sang harmony.

But Gaye could Bible read without skipping many words. Faye never got beyond "See Spot Run."

When Daddy Dolph was working away, one twin had to stay home with Mama Maye to hit her in the back if the asthma caught her. Mama Maye preferred the slaps of Faye to the knotted fist Gaye gave her. Faye stayed home from school and learned to cross-stitch and roll out whole families of gingerbread.

Gaye got the slopping and the milking and the schooling.

Half the time she went as her sister Faye three grades back. All she had to do was change rings and wear her hair ribbon on the right side. The other half she was Gaye, with green ring and the ribbon on the left. She could print for Faye's right hand, write joined hand for her left.

She knew she could pass Faye out of the second grade, herself out of the fifth, but the County wrote a law against thirty days of absence.

They both failed.

Daddy Dolph got mad and took them out when they reached thirteen.

They took turns staying home to hit Mama Maye and going to Nat's Store and Post Office to trade and get the medicines she ordered from afar.

What Gaye liked most about going was Nat's new radio, when his wife would let him play it. Gaye had a stub pencil to write down the verses she could catch. Her favorite was the Stanley Brothers on *The Farm 'n Fun Time.* She also liked the Wonder Horse who could count to ten while the fiddles played.

She begged Daddy Dolph for a radio.

"Satanish," he said.

"They's some hymns," Gaye said.

Faye started singing "Mother's Bible." Gaye moved in on the chorus.

"One hymn to close a full hour of the Devil," Daddy Dolph said.

Gaye saved up egg money and ordered pictures of Carter and Ralph Stanley letting their instruments rest, the Wonder Horse bowing his head to his hoof to count numbers. When she wasn't looking at them, she stored them in the hope chest she shared with Faye.

If Daddy Dolph was home, they both could go. They dressed alike and walked arm in arm. They drank identical pop. Ate identical peanuts.

Gaye did most of the talking. Faye did most of the smiling. At the store and, when Mama Maye felt like it, at meetings, wakes and funerals where they volunteered their voices and let people try to figure out which one was the prettiest.

At home they slept in the same bed across from their parents and never fought unless Gaye peed.

But Gaye knew there was a difference. She would see a strange paw track by the spring, think panther, and say, "Wonder what that is?"

"Dog," Faye would say.

Or Gaye would look at the rocks on the hillside and say, "Don't that look like Carter Stanley tunin' up?"

"Rock," Faye would say.

Mama Maye wished for a double wedding if the time ever came and identicals in the male line could be found. There was only one set around Copperhead and they were old and palsied.

Daddy Dolph wanted one twin to marry Rankin Womble, their neighbor. He had land and cows, but just a thumb and little finger on his right hand.

Gaye overheard them barter in the barn.

"Give Bossy's calf when she comes frash," Womble offered.

"Which one you wont?"

"Don't matter."

"Any boot?"

"Clairissie Combs said I could have her Thelma free," Womble said.

"Then I'd marry in a dark moon," Daddy Dolph said.

Gaye ran cried to Mama Maye who said she could do worse.

Gaye knew she'd better start looking. The June all-day-meeting-and-dinner-on-the-ground was coming up. She took pains to prepare for it.

She talked to Faye long about the crepe paper dresses they would wear.

"Blue?" Gaye asked.

"Red," Faye said.

At Nat's store Gaye chose three rolled packs of paper red as a woodpecker's head.

Faye turned some red packs over and over in her hands and then chose the blue of Mary's head rag in Mama Maye's Bible.

Gaye wanted to change, but Nat didn't have six blues.

At least the pattern Faye stitched was the same: square neck, princess sleeves, long waist ribbons and ruffles round the skirts.

They tried the dresses on and practiced smiling in the mirror. Gaye saw the red didn't go with her complexion. Faye wouldn't swap.

What paper was left over Mama Maye puckered into grave flowers.

On the Sunday of the meeting a red sky in the morning told of rain, but Daddy Dolph had already hired a truck and driver to transport Mama Maye who would not walk with asthma.

Faye and Gaye would not sit. They rode upright in the back to keep the dresses from crinkling. Faye in the right corner; Gaye in the left. Rankin Womble, in between, tried to flirt bounce against first one and then the other.

Faye smiled and threw up her hand to rank strangers. Gaye kept her hands to herself and looked.

Up on the gap, Mama Maye decorated her near and distant dead. Daddy Dolph counted tombstones to see which family had the most. Womble rubbed dirt from his mama's name.

Faye and Gaye looked at the crepe paper flowers and the other dresses and then lined up in the grove beyond the graves to sing. They had practiced hard on three songs, but too many singers came and the preachers let them show off only one. They chose "Satan's Pretty Pictures" after Rubygay Rose went first with "Fly 'Way Ole Glory."

Faye rushed the pauses. Gaye had to suck breath fast to follow.

The singing stopped and one preacher prayed long enough for a sermon. Gaye told Mama Maye they were going to walk down the lane to catch a breath of fresh air.

Mama Maye frowned but she couldn't rise from her bedspread

on the ground, and Daddy Dolph was roaming.

Arm in arm they passed through the graves children were falling over, through the graveyard gate, down a little knoll to the lane where men and backsliders congregated.

A few boys whistled but they weren't any better than Rankin Womble. Faye smiled but Gaye didn't even bother to turn her head sideways.

Around the first curve they met music makers who had come to pick for Jesus. Three strains of Baptists had banded against the Holiness to keep stringed instruments out of the graveyard. The music makers turned hellion and were playing hoedown.

Faye and Gaye stood in the middle of the road and hugged each other's waist and listened to "Rollin' in My Sweet Baby's Arms."

Then the fiddler winked at them with both his eyes and set out to play and sing "Idie Red, Idie Blue, I'm in love with Idie two."

Gaye felt a blush clash against her dress. Faye's looked good on blue.

"Idie Red, Idie Blue, can't put a saddle on a humpbacked mule," the fiddler sang.

The paper of Faye's waistband trembled. Gaye glanced down at her sister's right foot. It was wiggling. She let her left one pat too. But when her eyes rose she saw Daddy Dolph coming in full stride. Dancing to him was fornication set to music.

Gaye turned Faye haw before they could get a switching. They hurried back to the grove and listened past hunger to the preachers yell out glory.

The fiddler followed without his instrument. He hid behind a tall tulip tree directly above Mama Maye's bedspread and made eyes from one side of the tree, then the other.

Gaye got some good glimpses of his black curly hair, eyes blacker, and a chin dimple deep as Satan's.

Faye stared at him head on.

When the fifth preacher lost his voice, time was called for dinner on the ground. Mama Maye chose to spread with the Free Wills, though Daddy Dolph was partial to the Hardshells.

The fiddler braved up to join them. "I'm Dancey Viers an' I reckon this is Idie Red an' Idie Blue," he said.

"Faye an' Gaye," Mama Maye named them backwards.

"Pretty as a picture," he said.

"Pretty is as pretty does," Mama Maye said. But she handed him a fat breast of chicken.

With each nibble he winked.

"Seems to me I smell liquor," Daddy Dolph said to a sausage biscuit.

Dancey Viers just went on nibbling and winking.

"Lips 'at touch whiskey will never touch mine," Womble said and stood in Gaye's way so she couldn't get her share of the flutters. She got Womble's thumb and little finger wrestling crumbs.

When she bent the crepe paper, slow, to lift a wedge of devil's food cake, Gaye rolled her eyes in Dancey's direction and watched his moustaches grin over the pulley bone. Her knees went so weak she almost fell backwards.

Dancey waved Womble aside to let Faye and Gaye pull the bone. "Make a wish," he said and licked his moustaches.

The heat of his hams, inches away, bore through the paper to moist Gaye. She closed her eyes and wished for Dancey Viers.

She got the short end of the bone.

Gaye didn't know what Faye wished, but she didn't get him either. Before the second round of preaching could bring sweat, black clouds from the west opened and drenched the graveyard and the grove.

Faye grabbed the bedspread and ran to the truck for shelter.

Daddy Dolph carried what was left in the dinner box.

Gaye got the cane hand of Mama Maye. Rankin Womble got the free one.

Mama Maye would not be rushed.

Most of Gaye's dress melted. What didn't puckered out like red measles turned to boils. She was dyed past princess slip, past drawers.

Faye, dry, rode Daddy Dolph's lap in the cab.

Gaye got the bed and Rankin Womble tumbling at her.

When the truck bounced past the graveyard gate, Dancey Viers, naked to the waist, raised his pink shirt in the rain and waved it wild. "Can't put a saddle on a humpbacked mule," he yelled.

Gaye couldn't see what her sister did, but she waved back at him and kept on waving even after a curve took him away from her.

Daddy Dolph warned he'd unjoint their necks if they traipsed after a drunk fiddler.

Before they could disremember his wishes, Rankin Womble came to talk of cows and to add, as if it didn't matter, "Dancey Viers signed up for the Army, went away."

Gaye's mind held onto the chin that cradled the fiddle, the moustaches that danced.

One night Faye flopped an arm and a leg on her and moaned, "Dancey."

Gaye peed on her.

In the spring of the next year, their fifteenth, Daddy Dolph got word to come cut the trees on West Virginia.

Mama Maye would not budge. "Ye'll have to home come when ye can," she said.

Daddy Dolph gave Faye and Gaye a sermon before he left. "Don't paint," he said. "Don't smoke. Stay 'way from stranged instruments."

He looked them both in the face and then in Mama Maye's.

"Fiddler's overseas," Gaye said. She had heard it at Nat's.

"Keep ye drawers on. Ye legs crossed. And don't go car-ridin'."

He shook abominations into his head. "They's whorehouses on

wheels."

Faye and Gaye nodded that they knew.

"If youens start puttin' out, I'll unjoint some necks."

They took turns, Monday through Saturday, going to the store and post office. Faye got firsts. Gaye got Rankin Womble come to flirt and talk about his cows cutting up.

Mama Maye took him outside on the porch to put some air between them.

He rolled at Gaye his swimmy blue eyes that just missed being pink.

She went inside to practice "Get in Touch with God, Turn Ye Radio On."

Mama Maye had to tell Womble when it was time for him to go.

At the end of the first week, Gaye knew Faye was car-riding. She hummed songs hymnals hadn't given her, about blue moons over her shoulders and a dram glass set in her hand. And when Gaye sniffed Faye's going dress, she smelled gasoline.

"You car-ridin'?" she whispered to her in the dark.

Faye grunted and rolled over.

She asked her again in the morning. She just grinned and hummed pickup trucks.

At breakfast, Gaye said, "Mama, I thank Faye's car-ridin'."

Mama Maye looked up from her gravy and said, "Hursh ye evil mouth."

Gaye gathered proof on Tuesday. Cars and trucks slowed down, but when they saw the hair bow on the left side, they changed gears and went on.

By mid-June, Gaye knew Faye was putting out. Her comb had reddened. Her cheeks and lips looked paint-smeared. She smiled more than usual. She'd look at the kitten or Ole Bowser and grin wide-mouthed.

And her walk was different. She made dimples in her butt, and Gaye could tell her hips were spreading on her.

"You puttin' out?" Gaye whispered to her in the dark.

Faye hummed "Rollin' in My Sweet Baby's Arms."

"What's 'at?" Mama Maye coughed and said from across the room.

"New hymn," Faye lied.

"I thank Faye's puttin' out, Mama," Gaye said.

Faye pinched her. And the next morning, without warning, Mama Maye slapped Gaye so hard she brought nose blood.

That very day Faye came home without her hair ribbon and her ring. Lost them, she said. But she had found a pair of silk stockings and an angel food cake.

Mama Maye turned the stockings over and over in her hands and smiled. Then she and Faye ate right through the cake.

Gaye kept her mouth shut, but she twirled her green ring and wondered.

She decided to leave the ring and ribbon at home to see what would happen. On the way up the main road, the Bread Truck gave her a raisin cake to let him twiddle on her knees. He breathed hard and dropped her off on the curve before Nat's.

She caught half of *The Farm 'n Fun Time.*

On her way home the Mail Man waited just beyond the same curve. He gave her a seed catalog and some circulars to let him play gear shift between her legs.

She took her box of pretties from the hope chest to put the new gifts in. Her pictures of the Stanley Brothers and the Wonder Horse were gone.

She accused Faye of giving them to some whorehopper.

Mama Maye's hand across Gaye's face denied it.

When Daddy Dolph came home for a monthly weekend, he looked straight into both their faces and said, "Youens been puttin' out."

Faye started singing "My Jesus Has Broad Shoulders." Gaye harmonized.

Daddy Dolph seemed satisfied.

Gaye missed her Saturday, for Daddy Dolph went to Nat's to tell how hot it got in West Virginia. But on Tuesday, when the Wholesale Man hesitated, she threw up her hand and he scattered sundries to stop.

He turned his truck around and took her to the gravel pile. He gave her some Planter's peanuts and turned the radio on. While the Stanley Brothers were singing "He Will Set Yore Fields on Fire," he rolled on protection and poked around on her insides.

"Glad ye changed ye mind?" he asked when he had put his silly back in its hole.

She knew it wasn't the Wholesale Man, but she took the pound of bacon he gave home.

She handed it to Mama Maye. She turned it over and over, but she did not smile.

"Don't ye know what brangin' home the bacon means?" she asked.

Gaye didn't. Mama Maye slapped her winded and threw the hog meat at Ole Bowser.

It wasn't the Bread Truck either. "Been wontin' 'at for a long time," he huffed, as he rolled off his protection. He gave her a gross of Moon Pies. She ate every last one of them before she got home. Liked to have foundered.

The Pop Truck seemed likeliest. He moaned and groaned and carried on so she was sure she had found him, but he bit her left ear and whispered, "Gaye, you somethin.'"

She slammed his truck door and went home.

At supper the way Faye ate her kraut hinted pregnant. Gaye lost her appetite just watching her wallow it around in her mouth. Then Faye jumped up from the table and caught a gag in her printing hand and ran with it to the toilet.

"Dog Days," Mama Maye said.

"I wonder," Gaye said. "Sometimes I just wonder."

She checked Faye's dress and found it pouched out in the belly.

"You pregnant," she whispered to Faye that night.

Faye grunted.

"You knocked-up," Gaye whispered.

Faye rolled over.

The next morning Faye mixed kraut with her gravy and smiled her silliest and slapped out her tongue.

But she got her reward. She stepped on a rusty nail and had to stay home and listen to Womble brag about Bossy while Gaye did the gallivanting.

Gaye was running out of trucks, but she was going to spread till she found out who it was Faye put out to.

The Mail Man said, "You ain't like ye sister."

"How come?"

"She won't let me get past step-ins," he said.

The Bread Truck blew his horn. She told him to blow it out his nose.

The Wholesale Man waited beyond the curve. She prissed by the truck door that he fanned.

The one it was didn't even have a truck. He had a horse and from its back he whistled at her from the bushes above Sickle Curve.

She saw a little worn path leading up to the cliffs. She followed it.

Dancey Viers with his hands in Army pockets and no protection waited.

He led her to his playhouse, a little cave that had her pictures of the Stanley Brothers and the Wonder Horse that could count. And perched high on a dry rock was Faye's hair bow.

As he helped her downward to a bed of pine boughs, she saw Faye's red birthstone on his little finger. Before she could say who she was, her dress tail was touching her neck and he was plowing deeper than the others could.

"When you gone tell 'em?" he asked.

"Soon," she said. She caught his hams in her hands and helped him churn up glory.

When he was about to shake the needles from pine, she loosened her thighs and said, "I'm Gaye."

He missed a stroke.

"God Amighty," he said.

"Gaye," she said.

"I'm ridin' too high to stop," he moaned.

"You ridin' Gaye," she said.

"Least ways I'm ridin."

Her hips rose to greet what he could give.

After a second stand he kissed her on the right cheek and told her he'd been hiding out for months. That nobody knew but Faye and his mama.

"Hidin' from what?" she asked.

He wouldn't say. But he did say, "Day after tomar?"

She didn't say next day.

At the supper table, Gaye hummed the Stanley Brothers and said she'd seen their picture and two horses and a hair bow just like Faye's.

In bed, she whispered "Dancey" and threw an arm and a leg on Faye's belly.

The next morning Faye put rosin on the nail hole and hobbled out of the holler.

Gaye churned. Molded butter into rosebuds.

Womble came to pick blisters on his left hand and tell that Bossy had come fresh.

"Be somebody else frash soon," Gaye said.

Mama Maye stared brimstone.

"Got me new radio," Womble said.

Gaye played like she was listening to it and slapped her feet on the porch floor.

Come sunset, Mama Maye told Womble to go.

Gaye did the milking. Chopped wood. Cooked supper. Washed dishes.

Mama Maye looked down the holler. "My little girl's lost," she cried.

"I know where she's at," Gaye said.

Mama Maye breathed heavy three times to say say.

"Puttin' out to Dancey Viers in his love cave," she said.

Mama Maye choked on asthma. Gaye gave her three hard fists.

"He's acrost the waters," Mama Maye said.

"He's hidin' out. I seed him yesterday."

As soon as Mama Maye could breathe again, she said, "Go get Womble 'fore hit's dark."

Gaye climbed the hillside to fetch him. He had his radio on, but she wouldn't darken his door. She told him Mama Maye's need and pressed dimples in her butt to give him reason to hurry on their way down.

Mama Maye had not died. Gaye showed Womble how to hit her if she tried to. Then she lit the lantern and took it out of the dark holler and up the road to Sickle Curve. She thought how she'd ease up on them at it and make him choose which one would take his rides, catch his babies.

She climbed the little path and let the light of the lantern spread on nothing. The Stanley Brothers were gone. The Wonder Horse. The hair bow. The bine boughs had been burned. Her fingers sifted ashes.

Then her feet forgot they were bare. They bruised rocks to get back home.

She walked in on a honeymoon of fried chicken. The marriage license was spread out on the table with the pictures of the Stanleys and the horse.

Mama Maye was laughing and choking and crying all at the same time.

"It's about time," Gaye said and started to wash up their filthy dishes.

"'Bout time you went home," Mama Maye said to Womble.

He did.

Dancey and Faye got her bed. She made herself a pallet in the other room, but the door was open and she heard the springs squeak.

She coughed.

They squeaked louder.

She sang two verses of "He Will Set Yore Fields on Fire."

Mama Maye rolled over and hollered, "Gaye, you keepin' us from bed rest."

She listened till dawn to them try to keep the springs from spelling out what they were up to.

She wet her pallet and cried in it, benastied.

The next day they moved on to escape the U.S. Army and two stores he had robbed.

Gaye had to stay home every day.

She paled and talked to herself.

She hit Mama Maye's back and rubbed her own belly.

"Let's move to West Virginia," she pleaded when Daddy Dolph came home.

"Move ye mommie," he said.

"Ain't gone budge," Mama Maye said.

"See youens next month," Daddy Dolph said.

Every day Rankin Womble came to say how fat his calf was getting.

"They's somebody else 'at's gettin' fat," Gaye said.

Womble rubbed his belly. "Taters," he said.

"How's ye radio?" she asked.

"Hit's turnin' out pickin'."

She smiled to make his knees flap time.

Faye had been gone three months and a day when Gaye married Rankin Womble. Gaye was three months and two days gone herself.

Mama Maye moved up the hill to be with them. Gaye counted two mamas under one roof. One too many. Daddy Dolph sold the house and took Mama Maye to West Virginia.

Womble fed and bred and milked his cows. Gaye churned and listened to the radio, and she walked to Nat's every other day.

At Christmas a letter came for Mama Maye. It was marked Detroit, and on the left-hand side of the envelope were the initials F.V. Gaye opened it. It was a snapshot of a tiny baby. On the back of the picture was printed Faye Maye XO XO XO. She knew Faye's print.

In the spring Gaye gave birth to twin boys, five and one-half pounds, black curly hair, eyes blacker, and chin dimples deep as Satan's. She named them Carter and Ralph, and as soon as they were old enough to have the flaps of their blankets spread, she put bows in their hair and hired a Kodak to snap them.

On the back of the photo she wrote:

"They's a pitcher of ther dady."

P.S. Step before the lookn glass an kiss yeself for me."

She addressed the envelope: Mr. Dancey Viers
Genral Delivry
Detroit Mitchagan.

She never got an answer.

Heart Leaves

HEART LEAVES

When she was nine she bled. She daubed the flow with leaves and didn't wonder till later when the grainy wetness caught her by surprise. She was following the bells of the cows who had roamed into the woods and stubborned. She stopped to fondle rhododendron. The wetness came.

A bird's nest full of eggs could bring it on, the smell of heart leaves. But mostly rain. When thunder basefiddled heaven, her fingers traveled to her thighs to play.

Pearl Duty said it was dying. For five years Bethel kept hands from thighs. Unless it rained.

Then after Christmas recess, she glanced up from her speller to the back of the room and saw the eyelashes of the new boy dance. She crossed her legs and tried to think of *i* before *e.* But she died.

Pearl said Doll Newberry's daddy killed a man in West Virginia and that his mama kept hounds in their house on Cherry Mountain. But he rode a spotted horse and Pearl petted its mane.

Bethel swapped her front-row desk for a middle so she wouldn't have to strain.

Her mama and her daddy said the Newberrys were no count—that his daddy shot a branch walker and was serving time. But Doll smelled of all her nose had taught her of perfume.

He couldn't read. He couldn't spell. His talk was from tongues that hadn't learned from paper, but he could count in tens and he liked to hear the teacher tell of Abe Lincoln's eyes in lamplight. His ears and eyes followed Mr. Armentrout and history.

The teacher plagued him only once. The first day he was asked to stand and read. He sat and stared red-faced into the book.

At dinner recess, those who brought food brushed snow from the well box to spread biscuits and sugar cake, to open lard cans filled with cornbread and milk.

Doll unhitched his spotted horse from the woodshed and rode off.

Bethel slipped a gingerbread baby in his desk. From the corner of an eye she saw his fingers pick crumbs to his mouth.

The next day her desk had walnuts, hickory, hazel. She kept some for a love box she was building.

She gave up the games of children. A farmer in the dell ground his heels in a circle to follow her eyes aimed upward at Doll Newberry on the big rock above the schoolyard. At "Hi-ye-o, my derie-o," she broke circle and ran to the schoolhouse porch. She glanced upward. His nose and fingers were inspecting the winter sap of spruce. But he turned his face downward for her.

From then on all games were just children in a ring.

At little recess, at dinner, and at big, her eyes stalked happy when they could catch a patch of him.

If a storm came up at free time, the scholars could play seat games or stand on the porch and flirt with fever.

Bethel flirted with Doll who made eyes at the sky. She let her whole face feast on half of his. And when his eyes shifted slightly to contain her, he would sigh and shift his weight, but she could see his britches grow as her thighs tightened to hold the wetness in.

At books, she learned how his page-turning finger caught spit. How, when he thought no one was looking, another finger joined to tug at a thin moustache. How at spelling his britches would sag, his legs bow to catch the belly of a horse that wasn't there.

But at history his legs would tighten when the teacher told of frozen Delawares.

It was in a morning drizzle she first touched him. She lingered on the porch till she heard hooves splash. She went to the little cloakroom and waited.

Mr. Armentrout cracked the Bible for devotion just as Doll's shoulders filled the cloakroom door.

Bethel's hand, fluffing dryness to her hair, caught the damp wool of his mackinaw. His fingers, fumbling for buttons, brushed hers.

"They's courtin' in a cloakroom," she heard Pearl Duty say above the teacher's "it shall come to pass."

Doll's hands darted to his pockets.

She took her seat for morning singing. She felt her cheeks fry.

She dared peep at him over a grade of history. The rose of a blush spotted his neck.

In February she found an early violet blooming under a little rock that jutted out. She covered it from freeze at night, opened it to the thaw at day. And on the fourteenth she picked it and put it in a red valentine of her own making, a boy and girl on a spotted horse in the middle of a heart. The horse was pretty. She traced that. The boy and girl she put on it looked squatty.

She arrived at school early to slip it in his desk.

Her valentine came a day late, a bouquet of heart leaves tied with the bark of birch. All day long she breathed the sweetness of the gather. In geography she forgot all her capitals.

Mr. Armentrout kept her after school to talk low. She was supposed to go away free to Normal next year. Bethel lowered her eyes and watched her right foot tap out no.

On her way home she put a heart leaf in her bosom. She

hugged the bark of birches.

The next day, though a flurry made vague the horse's haunches, he rode the first grade in a circle around the schoolyard. When the last of five slid from the horse, Pearl Duty said, "When ye gone ride me an' Bethel?"

He nodded to Bethel. He pranced his horse to the well box. Her galoshes mounted. A hand swooped down to pull her for a side ride without a saddle.

She had made up how even her hair would flow. It would part in equal manes and tickle his neck as they rode off into the wilds.

But her hips kept the rest of her busy holding on. His left arm crooked for the same purpose. It gave her too much of a circle for bouncing.

When he let her down on the well box, she thought she felt her hair brush his face.

The long thaw came. He was absent more than present. The Government couldn't force him. He was over sixteen and they had his daddy. He had to stay home to plow.

Bethel smelled despair in the chalk, in the nests of mud-daubers, in the overripe sweat of feet.

At home she paled and mumbled. Her mama boiled her spring tonics. Rolled rosin pills.

At school she kept her head on her desk. But she wouldn't miss a day in case he came.

He came for three rainy days in a row.

She left letters in his desk. He left in hers an Indian baby doll whittled from the sweet scented root of pine.

The last week in April he didn't come a single day.

She languished so that Mr. Armentrout sent her home with a note. She tore it up and stayed in the woods listening to the cow bells and talking to red buds.

Though the last day of school was sunny, he came for his

report card. She knew it would be fail. He could come back for two more years if he wanted to.

Hers said pass, with no note for Normal. She could not come back.

Into his hands she placed pressed flowers and, for old time's sake, a fresh heart leaf.

In her desk was a bird's egg necklace, all blue and rounded to perfection. He rode off on his spotted horse before she could show him the neck it prided.

The first week away from school seemed longer than Moses' trip her mama made her read her every day. When Bethel came across a word she didn't know, she'd whisper Doll and lift her eyes toward Cherry Mountain and wonder what his hands and eyes were doing five miles away in wilderness.

As a child she had fought sleep to catch fireflies or try to peep the dusky eyes of whippoorwills. Now she complained of aches and went to bed early. Katydids sawed their itch; night birds swelled their throats. They blended with her dreams, wide-eyed and closed, of Doll and their twelve children who would escape snakebite and fever to grow up to take his face. When a storm came up at night, she flailed love for him into the featherbed.

She asked to go herbing, but her mama and her daddy wouldn't let her. Gallivanting they called it. They pointed out how Canady Crabtree lollagagged and ended up with a woods-colt at fourteen.

In late May she got to wear her necklace to a graveyard meeting to decorate her mama's dead. In early June to decorate her daddy's. She didn't catch a glimpse of Doll. His dead, she reckoned, were down in West Virginia.

When she could escape her mama's one good ear, she whispered to a schoolmate, "Seen Doll?"

Sardis Hess had seen him at the Jockey Grounds swapping

the spotted horse for a mule.

Nez Wampler saw him digging May Apple root.

Pearl Duty said she saw him almost every day, but Bethel knew different.

At home she helped her mama in the garden. Found the cows and drove them home. Milked and churned. Read the kin of Moses past the Promised Land.

In early July the oldest cow Piedy butted rails from the fence and roamed up the mountain. Cover and Cloudy followed. Her daddy walked the pasture fence to mend it. And though a red sky warned of rain, Bethel was sent to hunt the cows.

Two miles up the mountain she heard Piedy's old-timely bell clank tin. Another mile, the happy ring of Clover, like a hand-shook dinner bell. Cloudy wore a little brass one made for goats, a tinkle that hinted Christmas. Cloudy could not be told; but with the tin of Piedy in front and the iron of Clover in the middle, Bethel imagined the tiny bell baby out of the sound.

A half-mile away she could say what they were up to. The regular ring of walk. The unpatterned pause and ring of grass eating. The twisting side rings as their necks fought for buds. The more frantic clapper when they nudged away flies.

She knew a storm was brewing, for their bells had become flaps of fear, hanging quiet for thunder.

She let them hide so she could follow another sound—the high whine of gee, the fall of haw, the base of whoa that came from a spur on the ridge above her.

She came to a clearing. She parted rhododendron to see Doll, naked to the waist, follow a black mule through corn rows. She caught the slight nod of his head right with the gees, left with the haws. The lift of chin upward for the whoas. She counted the knobs of muscles on his arms and back. The brave tremble of his chest.

She held her sides and rocked against faint. And when her

knees stretched they could hold her, she answered her lips' say of go.

He stopped the mule in midfield. He looked to the black clouds in the west, where the best storms came. A sudden breeze gathered leaves and turned them white.

She walked up beside him and said, "Ye ain't heard no bells?"

The belly of God rumbled. Dull lightning streaked the western sky.

"Best get 'fore hit pores," he said. He unhooked the mule and led it into the woods. She followed, around the spur on a small path that came to cliffs that jutted out to make a cave.

He tied the mule to a limb that elbowed inward for the shelter.

On rocks were whittled objects, dried and drying herbs, nuts from last year's swell. Her valentine in a high dry place.

He pointed to a bed of pine boughs. "To dream time 'way," he said.

She lay down on the bed and breathed the sweetness.

Thunder rolled. Lightning quickened.

He lay down beside her. He nibbled a heart leaf from her bosom. His lips played juice-harp on her breast, minnowed her belly.

She smelled the summer in him. She kissed the sweet lay of hair on his belly—up through navel to the little knob that said three ribs were passed, and then to the dark thickets that grew on both hills the nipples made, up to the ponds of collarbones where she lipped his salt. Then the ears that caught and held the seed of hay.

She kissed the lower lip in its tremble, the upper in its spread of joy, the whole mouth for the jerk his belly gave to her thighs that knew to open, knew to close.

"You killin' me," he said.

She sucked growth into his moustaches.

He rolled over on his back to let his muscles jerk. She waited for the apples on his shoulders to say fall. Then her chin caught the cup of a shoulder blade and her left hand babied navel.

The rain came down in heavy sheets.

He turned over to greet her snuggle.

"Let's die again," she said.

He straddled her to help them.

She ground her hips sideways and squeezed until the sweet hurt came.

"You killin' me," he said.

Her hips rose to meet the ride.

He slept. Through thunder. Through gully washes.

She watched the two butt dimples rise and fall with his breathing. The storm darkened them from her eyes. Her fingers traced them through down.

He woke to breathe the sweet sourness sleep had fed him.

When a rainbow told them to, they rose to put on clothes. Doll reached out a hand to try to rake the color in. He settled for the new green that rain had given wildflowers.

She heard the clink of Piedy's tin, the clear ring of Clover, the tink of Cloudy.

"Day after tomar?" she asked.

He nodded.

"Noon?"

He nodded.

She gathered the cows and switched them into chimes. She laid her plan. She would cow hunt every other day on Cherry Mountain. She would stifle with rags and clappers of the cow bells. She would tie Piedy to a tree. Clover and Cloudy would linger beside her. She would slip all three forbidden winter hay at their milking to make up for lost graze.

She lied to her daddy that she had found the cows on Abner's Gap.

Her eyes were closed before the washed sky could blacken.

Her thighs gathered feathers to pillow the burn past bruise into memory.

She woke to disappointment. Her daddy took one look at Piedy's tail and said, "Cuttin' up." He took her to a known bull in the valley. The silly daughters stuck their heads over the yard gate and mooed till milking time.

Bethel was fitful. Day after tomorrow would be delayed, for that night her daddy did the milking.

She sat on the front porch and read her mama the psalms of David and tried to catch the harps in her mind.

She couldn't hide the cows till Thursday evening's milking.

When they didn't come home by morning, her daddy said she would have to go find them. Once she was out of his sight, she followed a straight path up Cherry Mountain.

At the cave, the pine boughs were gone. In their place was a full bed of moss with blue-eyed grass and heart leaves duly spread. She let her face take their tickle.

She walked to the field. It was finished. She heard no gees, no haws.

She returned to the cave and prayed for him to come.

She rose to measure her shadow for noon.

She heard the nose of the black mule splutter, the click of Doll onward.

She quickly spread the heart leaves into pattern.

Her hand trembled when it helped him knot the strap of the bridle round the limb.

She told him how her daddy and Ole Pied had kept her from him.

They lay down together. Soreness made them gentle. His hands played pity-pat on her thighs. Her fingers forgot fumbles as they loosened his belt to trace down. She smelled the drip of work in him.

New blood drove away the blue from bruises.

They let the moss lip them, let the heart leaves slow impressions. Their thighs obeyed without a crop of thunder.

The day after tomorrow was Sunday. Her daddy would not violate the Sabbath for field work, but he would claim an ox in the ditch to hunt cows. She would have to hide them Sunday, see him Monday.

She led home the bewildered Piedy. Her bell, obedient to the fasting, told tin. Clover iron. Cloudy brass.

She milked them. Not much.

Stole them hay. A lot.

Her daddy deemed the bull's topping hadn't taken. On Sunday he led Piedy placid to the valley where the bull turned up his nose.

Yet Bethel's plan worked Monday and for three weeks till her daddy sold Piedy. Said she taught them all to roam and stubborn. They were going dry.

Bethel tied Clover to a tree, but Cloudy traipsed home without her and lolled her head over the yard gate.

After three days away from Doll's eyes, she risked death.

She waited till snores told her she could gather dress from bed post. She held her breath for the count of fifty footfalls.

Bushes hugged for her hair. Sawbriars tried to tangle feet.

She slapped and kicked at thickets.

By midnight she crossed the field she knew. Then a tobacco patch. A stream. A garden. She saw his cabin stilled in moonlight.

She inched her way to the one window. She saw the face it gave her back — eyes rounded past recognition, lips pouted with fear. She heard the house hounds throat their warning. She jerked reflection away and waited behind the dahlias for what the dogs' teeth or Doll could give her.

She got Doll, his long fingers pushing at the noses of the dogs.

He took her elbow and they walked beyond the voice of his

mother asking who.

The dogs, wagging now, smelled her out. She gave them her hands. They purposed tails and noses for night roam.

She told of the thwart. His arms answered she could count on him.

When the dew divided them, she said, "Come to me."

He came every other night through August. She held him under the crabapple tree, or when thunder squeezed the mountains into awe, in last year's corn shucks in the crib.

Once her mama rose to feel the bed and wonder where she was. Bethel claimed sleepwalking had taken her by surprise.

Her thighs caught wonder three months without daubing. She told Doll she was big. He replanted to be sure.

Her daddy found them and prized them apart before frost could. He threatened death and prison.

Bethel clutched her dress to her and said, "You kill three."

Her daddy lifted his right hand to the heavens and declared her dead.

"Go," he said. "With 'at woodscolt in your belly."

She had only the one dress on her back. Her mama later slipped her others with love notes in the pockets.

They didn't marry. Doll and his mama didn't like the State. She asked his mama's blessing. She smiled through snuff and gave it in wide wink.

They stayed with her till the State gave back his daddy. Then they moved to a higher mountain where she taught wild flowers to grow in her yard, where he tilled fields and caught the bees in trees and told them to make honey.

The pregnancy was false. And every one thereafter. She would swell, but the egg would not ripen on her.

She made up the names and lives of twelve who escaped snakebite and fever to grow up to take his face. Doll would lie quiet in bed to listen to her tell what the children of her mind had done that day.

She grew too fat. He grew too thin. And they learned to snore many nights away. But when a storm would come, she'd rustle the bed clothes and turn to him.

And he'd say, "You gone kill me."

She did, in the flood of '52. At a clap of thunder, as he spent, he gave a gurgle she hadn't heard before. Then he lay heavy upon her.

She turned him over, and through lightning, she courted the skin time had blotched. Her lips traced the gray hairs to the knob that said three ribs were passed. Her arms cradled him till dawn.

She rose to see a rainbow. Her hands reached out to try to rake it in, but they settled on the new green rain had given.

She told them all—the flowers, the children, the bees—and, on her weak way down the mountain, the Queen's Lace, the Pennyroyal, heart leaves.

Myrtie's Salvation

MYRTIE'S SALVATION

She didn't know what denomination she was, but she knew she had been baptized and born again and that she had to fight every waking breath to hold onto both of them. Some people could just ease into salvation. Her mama heaped coals of fire on the heads of sinners by smiling into their faces, but Myrtie had a hard time. When somebody badmouthed her or she got her finger caught in a gate latch, she had to swallow fast to keep from saying "Sumbitch." She often woke herself up cussing out a string of oaths. But she figured that if Jesus had her every waking breath, she didn't have to lay her night thoughts on the altar. Sometimes she woke her husband Stirt up and he'd say, "Myrtie, you losin' yore religion," and she'd say, "Praise be His holy name," and fall right back.

Holding onto what she had was easier before they moved to Copperhead. The old holler on Red Sow Branch had only two houses. Her mama that smiled at sin lived in one of them. Copperhead had many hollers of houses that led to a hardtop road with more, and on to Nat's Store and Post Office. With Stirt at the sawmill and no garden to speak of, she and Stirt's children by Wife Number One had time to stop.

The first day she passed by more sin on front porches than she had seen in all her life on Red Sow Branch. Radios threw out love and wine in pickup trucks. She rushed the children by. But when the screen door slapped them inside Nat's, she knew she'd have to work overtime to hold onto what she had.

Big Buster, who could read, pointed to a homemade sign and said, "No sin permitted on these premises," but she could sniff it out. Rat poison and fertilize and galvanized tubs. Big Buster and Little Sadie thrived on it. They sashayed up and down eating green gum drops.

"Where'd youens come from?" Nat asked from the store's one rocker.

"Red Sow," Big Buster said.

A skinny woman in a straight back giggled.

Nat grinned. His wife Alafair smirked behind the counter.

Myrtie felt mortification take her face in blush.

Big Buster tugged her out of it and to the post office side where he pointed out pictures of swarthy men that had robbed, killed and raped the Government. One had a special poster to himself with more names than she could count.

"Sidney Harelip," Big Buster read. "Angel Eyes, The Man, Satan Sid, A Caution."

"They Lord God," she said.

The poster gave only three of his pictures, one with a right cheek, one with a left, and one head on. From the bread rack he looked like Stirt, but with busy burnsides and a curly moustache. From the little post office window, he had the long hair of Jesus Knocking at the Gate. Square dab on, he was the meanest "sumbitch" she'd ever seen, swimmy eyes, dog-gnarl lips and chin bones sharp as a reaphook.

"He's in Top Ten," Nat said and buttoned on his radio.

"Number One," Alafair said and buttoned it off.

"He's wanted the most," Big Buster said.

Myrtie felt a chill run up the bushes of her spine.

Little Sadie took her by the hand to the pictures tacked onto the back of the store door — a two-headed heifer, an eight-legged cow, two babies joined at the haunches and a man up to the middle where a woman set in with painted lips and ear bobs.

Her mama once had a cow with eight working tits, but Myrtie said, "They Lord God."

She wondered what sins the fathers had visited upon them.

The pictures from both sides were drawing salvation from the very corners of her eyes. She tried to focus straight ahead on Cow Chow, Pig Starter, and when her eyes did roll gee or haw, she batted hard to hold onto what she had.

The truck came from the U.S. Mail.

Big Buster and Little Sadie lined up with strangers on the post office side and waited for Nat to open the little window and shake his head yes or no.

There was no mail for Stirt's house

On their way home, they guessed the crimes of Mr. Number One.

"Tore 'im up some school girls," Little Sadie said.

"Cut throats on a whole ranch a cowboys," Big Buster said.

"Robbed mailboxes," Myrtie said.

The next day Big Buster squinted up close to read so they wouldn't have to guess. They had all been right, everything from mail fraud to rape was on his list.

Big Buster read the descriptions, but only four stayed the same on all his shapes: West Virginia, six-feet-two, eyes of gray, and a long blue ape scar on the left side of his belly.

Myrtie puzzled how the Government got him to strip down. The three pictures didn't show him below the neck and she'd never heard of an ape scar, but when she closed her eyes she saw a big blue gash three feet long.

"How'd ye like meet up with 'at on a dark night?" Nat asked.

"I'd rock 'im," Big Buster said.

Myrtie couldn't say what she'd do. Her heart jerked her tongue. She crossed over to the other side.

No letter came.

On their way home, they guessed new crimes.

"He hacks a heads off babies," Little Sadie said.

"Slits necks on women an' dranks the blood," Big Buster said.

"Robs gardens," Myrtie said.

Until they ran out, they packed a face from a Wanted Man home with them every day and made up his life. Then Big Buster would thumb through the pictures to see who was right. He and Little Sadie grumbled when Myrtie got forgeries mixed up with fornications. She started keeping her best guesses to herself.

The children could throw the faces away, but they went to bed with Myrtie. The three Mr. Number One had got all jumbled and she'd toss and turn and moan and cuss.

"Myrtie, you losin' yore religion fast," Sirt said.

"Mr. Number One," she said.

Stirt thought she was leading him on and bruised her into the featherbed.

One day while Big Buster was reading a Wanted Man that had gagged a postmistress and tied her up to a live potbellied stove, the screen door slapped slow and Myrtie turned her head and there he stood—swimmy gray eyes, dog-gnarl lips and chin bones sharp as a reap hook.

She elbowed Big Buster's ribs, but he frowned and turned right back to his reading. Little Sadie was salvaging candy wrappers from the coal bucket. Myrtie had to hold what she knew inside.

"Where's The Fox been?" Nat asked.

A new name. A new shape—chin beard and a white cap with a pistol stitched on its bill.

"West-by-God-Virginia," he said.

She scrunched into the feed and fertilize corner.

"Bought me a truck load a monkeys from a roadside zoo," The Fox said and opened him a red pop. "Got me a room full of 'em."

Big Buster and Little Sadie walked right up to him and fronted his thighs.

"What ye wont with a room a monkeys?" Alafair asked.

"Show folks where 'ey come from," The Fox said.

"'Ey come from acrost the waters," Big Buster said. The Fox rested his bottle. Red stains rimmed his mouth. "West Virginia," he said.

Myrtie felt her knees take weak trembles.

"I seed 'em in geog'phy," Big Buster said.

"I wont see 'em" Little Sadie said.

"Ten cents a head. Fifteen for two," The Fox said.

"Look a monkey in a face ye'll become one," Lilly Clifton said from her straightback.

"Monkey see, monkey do," Alafair said.

"Aman," Lily said.

The Fox winked at Nat, but Myrtie caught the last of the flutter and almost fainted.

Little Sadie found Myrtie's hand in the dark corner and pulled. "I want see 'em monkeys," she whined.

Myrtie looked at her hard and yanked her out crying before the mail truck came.

Myrtie tried to get them to guess who The Fox was, but Little Sadie pouted and threw gravel at her. Big Buster, full of geography, said that The Fox didn't know his ass from a hole in the ground.

Little Sadie asked Stirt if she could have a dime to see Fox's monkeys.

Stirt cut a hickory switch.

She cried and danced out why and Stirt told her. " 'Em monkeys just to draw moonshine trade. Use to have a polly bird got drunk an' talked tongue."

"I wont see the polly bird," Little Sadie cried.

Stirt gave her the switch on the calves of her legs.

Big Buster hid under old shucks in the corncrib.

"Myrtie, you run around, you run around. Swear to God, how you run around." He waved hickory at her.

"I know who he is an' where he's from," she said.

Stirt wouldn't hear. "If you take my youngens see 'at blackguard, I'll tan yore hide an' send ye home."

He had returned his first wife to her mama.

Myrtie didn't dream that night, but she played like she did. When Stirt got sound, she whispered ape babble in his ear.

He raised his head from the pillow. "Myrtie?"

She puffed out sleep through mouth and nose.

When he got sound again, she whispered, "Sumbitch."

And she made runny gravy for his breakfast sop.

At the store she kept her ears and eyes open.

One day Lily said The Fox was from afar and looked like he might have served time.

Myrtie faced the poster of Mr. Number One. The resemblance held.

Nat said The Fox was one of them. That books had turned him curious.

The face of the left cheek softened.

"He's a no-heller. 'At much I know," Lily said.

Nobody disputed her word.

"Dresses 'em monkeys up like Christians," Lily said.

"Ought be a law," Alafair said.

Nat buttoned the radio on and found sin through static.

"Said he's gone name one for ever soul on Copperhead," Lilly said. She made the front legs of her straightback knock on the floor.

"Blastphemes the Holy Ghost," Alafair said.

"Pays 'is debts," Nat said, "cash an' carry." He turned the radio's sound up higher.

" 'Em monkeys done marked Bugle Ann Lambert's baby," Lily

said loud. "Got a tail four-five anches long. Head's so tiny Bugle won't open the flaps on its blanket."

Until the schoolhouse opened doors, Big Buster and Little Sadie daily wished they could see the monkeys dressed up like Christians and the baby with a tail and a tiny head.

"Ast ye daddy," Myrtie said.

"Wish in one hand," Little Sadie said.

"Shit in t'other," Big Buster said.

A new Wanted Man came, but without Big Buster she couldn't tell what he had done.

She left him for the new pictures The Fox gave Nat to go between the babies and the heifer, three monkeys that had become men.

" 'Ey come from Bible days," Nat said.

" 'Ey come from Hell," Alafair said.

Myrtie studied them up close—"The Peeking Man, Ole Neander, and Mr. Crow Man"—and then turned to the nearest face.

"They Lord God," she said and nodded acquaintance.

Alafair tore a picture from her Bible and nailed it over the one The Fox had brought. It was Jesus Walking on the Waters. But it wouldn't cover all three and Mr. Crow Man's nose and mouth pooched out from the right foot of Jesus.

Myrtie looked at Jesus and then at the store men. She shook her head sideways. She looked at Mr. Crow Man's nose. She shook her head up and down.

The next day Jesus was on the bottom. Bible clouds topped the Monkey Men. Bible waters bottomed them.

Nat turned the radio on and went outside to pump a miner some gas.

Alafair buttoned the music off and ripped the Monkey Men down and threw them into the coal bucket that served as spittoon.

Nat didn't let on he knew when he came back in. He hummed songs the radio had lent him.

Alafair's eyes tried to turn him into a salt block.

Myrtie waited till the crowd swelled. When everybody was drinking pop and arguing over where they came from, she bent over and jerked the picture from the bucket. She turned toward feed and fertilize and with one flick of the hand put it inside her bosom.

She hurried home without waiting for mail. She got her box of pictures from the chest of drawers. She put the Monkey Men in the middle of the bed. Pictures of her kin on one side. On the other, the Sunday School cards the Free Wills had given Little Sadie.

She didn't recognize the Bible Men. Essau, hairy top to toe, seeped in her brain and reminded her a little of the Wanted Men, without lamplight from Heaven to set their heads off, but she couldn't hold onto him.

The other side was easy. The Peeking Man's head looked enough like her grandpappy's to be his twin. Ole Neander had her mama's chin, and she had glimpsed the parts of Mr. Crow Man every day of her life.

She looked at cousins, first and removed. Mouths. Noses. Foreheads low. The spitting images froze her. She couldn't remember frying up supper.

That night she dreamt men from afar dug up the graves of her kin and cut their heads off for a Kodak. She screamed damn and sumbitch.

"Myrtie, you losin' yore religion fast," Stirt said.

"Praise be His holy name," she said and tried to fall right back. But all night long the faces of her kin grinned by her. Big Buster and Little Sadie, dwarf Peekings, threw green apples at her and laughed.

When the first crack of dawn came through the curtain, Stirt turned over to make the springs squeak. She looked him in the face and almost fainted. His ear and cheek belonged to Ole Neander.

As soon as he left for the sawmill and the children for school, she looked at herself in the mirror. Paint had never touched her lips, but what she saw made her charge up a tube of tangee. And what The Fox drug in to Nat's that day made her charge some rouge to go with it.

She was in a circle around Nat's rocker and The Fox stooped to turn the pages of a whole book of pictures. A little tadpole came up for air and crawled out on marshy land where it became a frog and a snake and, as the pages turned, nasty birds flew over jungles and lizards big as log trucks gobbled up tree tops— and on and on until a little monkey grew into a big one and The Peeking Man and Ole Neander and Mr. Crow Man hunkered in hides and stood upright. Before it all ended the tadpole became the mail man that slapped the screen door and broke up the circle.

"And 'at's where we all come from," the Fox said.

"Ain't no monkey in my tree," Alafair said.

"I come from the Bible," Lilly said.

The Fox looked straight at Myrtie and scratched his ribs with both hands and winked.

She robbed three mailboxes on her way home. The circulars were the same, a lipspread family walking hand-in-hand toward a steeple. She put them in the box with her other pretties.

Then, for the mirror, she opened wide her eyes. They belonged to frogs. She closed them. On the lashes way down, she saw a lizard wink.

Her right hand trembled when it applied the paint to lips, cheeks.

When she finished, she winked. Mrs. Crow Man winked back at her.

She straightened her spine and practiced smiling, but with each pucker or spread, the book's pictures peeped at her. She covered the mirror with a blanket.

She let her back hump into its place.

Stirt brought home a mess of frogs for supper. She had to fry them up or risk flogging. When the meat hit the hot lard and twitched, she saw little people waist down jigging in Hell.

Big Buster and Little Sadie greased their faces. Myrtie fasted and hummed "Froggie Went a-Courtin' and' He Did Ride, Uh-Huh."

Stirt noticed her lips and cheeks and said, "Myrt, you done lost yore religion."

"We's all frogs," she said.

Big Buster laughed, but Little Sadie's feelings were hurt.

That night Myrtie bit Stirt's ear and quoted Under-the-Root.

Stirt prized himself against the wall.

The next morning she doubled-coated her lips and cheeks without looking into the mirror and went to take everwhat the store and post office could throw out at her.

It was empty, except for Alafair and Lily.

" 'Ey's all gone monkey huntin'," Alafair said.

"Somebody turned 'em monkeys loose," Lily said.

"Ought send 'at Fox to the penitentiary," Alafair said. "Ought be a law."

"County's writin' up one," Lily said.

Myrtie got no mail.

She stole a muskmelon on her way home. She sat under a cucumber tree to eat. She looked up for monkeys in the limbs. She saw only what she reckoned was squirrels.

She knelt to drink water from her spring. She caught a glimpse of herself and shivered.

Buster and Sadie came home from school full of monkey talk.

"'Ey's mixin' with the squirrels," Little Sadie said.

" 'Teacher says 'em fellers grow so big up North 'ey throw women off a tops a steeples," Big Buster said.

"We's all monkeys," Myrtie said and looked at them long.

"You done gone stare-crazy," Big Buster said and took his geography to the crib.

Little Sadie hid under the bed until Stirt came home and yanked her out and the blanket off the mirror to slick down his hair.

Myrtie walked backwards and put the blanket up again. "If we's human, the woods is full of 'em," she said.

Stirt backhanded her hard on the mouth. He went out into the yard to whisper with Big Buster. Little Sadie followed.

Myrtie tasted blood. She went to bed and covered up her head. All night long she heard monkeys clawing at the window and sniffing at the door.

"May's well get up an' let dem fellers in," she yelled through covers across the room, where Stirt was sleeping with the children.

They whispered.

She sang what she knew of "Monkey Chased the Weasel."

Big Buster laughed. His daddy slapped him. He cried.

Little Sadie cried. Her daddy slapped her. She quieted.

Stirt layed off work the next day to go fetch her mama to cook.

Myrtie lay in bed. She watched her little mama monkey play around in pots and pans.

"Where'd I come from, mama?" she asked.

"Red Sow," her mama monkey said.

"Where'm I gone, mama?"

"Hell if ye don't change ye ways."

"Where you gone, mama?"

" 'At golden city four-square."

"Whad a monkey say to the baboon, mama?"

She didn't know.

"Said ye ain't got no tail atall," Myrtie told her.

Her little mama monkey shook her head and smiled and heaped up coals.

Stirt brought three gray-tails home for supper.

Her mama monkey stewed the squirrels in gravy.

When they sat down to eat, Myrtie said from her bed, "Youens eatin' our kin."

Little Sadie went outside to throw up.

The others lost what stomach they had.

"If 'ey don't catch 'em thangs soon I'm gone home," her mama monkey said.

" 'Ey done give up on catchin' 'em all," Big Buster said.

"Woods is full a 'em fellers," Myrtie said.

Her mama monkey pushed the table away. "'Gone home," she said.

"Take her with ye." Stirt pointed to Myrtie.

"Too old to take back," her mama monkey said. But she gathered up Little Sadie and Big Buster and they risked dark jungles toward Red Sow.

Stirt pulled Myrtie's covers off. " 'Ey's cages for people like you," he said.

"Monkey see," Myrtie said.

"Ye ain't no earthly use to nobody," he said.

"Monkey do," she said.

"Gone give ye to the State," he said.

The big black hairs on his hands sparkled in the lamplight. She looked him in the face. Ape hairs hugged for his throat.

He bruised her into the featherbed.

Then he tied her hands and feet and drug her to the mirror.

"Goddamn rip," he said.

She couldn't tell. Her eyes were closed.

He drug her to the corn crib. Locked the door.

He came back once in the night to gag her from singing

snatches from Nat's radio, but he didn't see that her bare feet were free under last year's shucks.

By morning her hands were loose, too, but she kept the gag in her mouth and her hands behind her when Stirt peeped through the slats.

"Gone get the papers," he said.

"Hellion," he said. "Bitch."

When she saw that he had cleared the first curve, she kicked two slats loose and crawled out. She knew what she had to do.

She walked mountain paths through huckleberries. Gone. Through elderberries. Gone. Through paw-paws ripe. She sat to eat her fill. She took some for the pouch her dresstail made.

She heard a double-barrel roar for squirrels or monkeys.

She walked on. Through cleared land. Corn new-shucked. Through tobacco cut.

She came to the house with the sign of money.

She unlatched the gate.

She held her dresstail of paw-paws in one hand. With the other she knocked. She heard scratching. Chatter. But no steps.

She knocked again. No steps. She thought of four miles wasted.

She tried the door knob. It turned. The door creaked. She snuck inside.

Her eyes squinted out the sun.

The monkeys were to home.

Black, brown, two gray.

Naked and Christian.

One strapped around the belly, three free.

Two daddies. One mama. One baby.

She stood still as death and looked them in their faces. They nodded acquaintance.

The little gray one nursed her baby. Her tits were tiny white grapes. Baby's mouth missed. Mama took a grape in her hand

and tested it for milk. She guided the grape into baby's mouth.

Baby sucked while mama looked its head for lice. She found one. She lifted it to her mouth and smacked.

Baby pulled hard. Mama bit it on the nape. Baby behaved.

Baby sucked while mama looked its head for lice. She found one. She lifted it to her mouth and smacked.

Big brown scratched his rump and threw Myrtie a kiss.

"Shag-nasty," she said, but with her free hand she threw it back to him.

Big black jumped toward her as far as the strap would let him. He hissed at her through yellow teeth.

"Boo on you," Myrtie said. She cupped a hand over her mouth to catch a giggle.

Little gray clutched for her puch. She handed her a paw-paw. She held it in both hands and nibbled. When her lips puckered in the goodness, she broke into chatter.

Myrtie knelt and let the paw-paws drop. The free monkeys circled her and tasted. She handed big black his share.

Mama gave baby its wad.

The monkeys smacked. Chattered. Danced.

And she rose to let her own toes tap.

She didn't hear him enter, but when her eyes caught the blue ape scar on his naked belly she didn't flinch.

" 'Ey like paw-paws," he said. The scar grew with his loss of breath, coiled inward for its gather.

The monkeys paused for the boom of a shotgun a ridge away.

The scar moved from the corner of her eye to the door. "Gone to West Virginia where 'ey ain't no laws," he said.

"Need me a ride 'is very day," she said.

"Where to?"

"Rocks an' mountains," she said.

She took his silence as an offer. She helped him crate monkeys and moonshine for the truckbed. She got to ride the cab for the first time in her life. She knew she should lay low, but she looked straight ahead at bushes slapping the windshield.

Off dirt and onto hardtop, the truck sliced the hot air into breeze. She put her right hand out the window to catch it. She waved backwards to the red leaves, the yellow. "Gone where the weather suits my clothes," she told them.

Between the say of gears she looked into the side of his chin beard. She nodded she was beholding.

"Where've I seed you at?" he asked without turning his reaphook.

She threw her head back so far the cartilage of her throat hurt. She laughed its way back down, in three little blasts of air. "I've knowed ye since time."

The muscles of his arms bunched into knots to help him around a curve. He cleared his throat in a cough and darted gray eyes in her direction.

"Gone hep ye clean through West Virginia," she said.

"Do what?"

"Rob mailboxes. Steal garden fruit." She made bars of her fingers to hide the blush of her face.

On a smooth stretch of road, she heard the monkeys claw and chatter. "Listen dem youngens, I wisht ye would. 'Ey run around, 'ey run around, Lord God how 'ey run around."

"What say?" he said.

"Whole woods is full," she said and pointed to the rocks the road was out through. "Swangin' on possum grapes. Weightin' down burshes."

"Where you from anyhow?" he asked.

"Hell, I reckon." She reached over to touch the blue scar that stretched with his gut.

He slapped her hand away. Swerved the truck left. Missed a forty-foot drop by a hair.

"Whee! Make 'at muffler roar." Her feet slapped giddy-up.

The crates in back stopped walking.

"Reckon 'at baby needs ninny?" she asked.

His head crawled into his neck and his hands squeezed the wheel to go faster.

"Roll on, buddy," she said and laughed through nose and mouth.

When they came to the State Line, he drove off the road on a curve and braked.

"We done got there?" she asked.

"You have to walk acrost," he said. "White slavery."

She winked that she knew both the law and the ways around it.

His hand, in tremble, helped her figure out the silver handle on the door.

Her bare feet felt the bruise of gravel. The ooze of tar.

She cleared the curve. Spraddled the white line and waited.

The motor raced for runego.

She raised her right hand high to flag him down, but he swerved around her.

The bed rack swayed from and then toward the next curve.

She stood stone still till the birds got back their song, the river in the valley had its say.

Her shoulders refound their hump. But she didn't look back.

Two coal trucks rattled past her.

Her feet chased the warmth of tar to find what lay beyond the next curve.

The fall of sun did not scare her. Nor the deep woods, which she took for night travel.

"Ain't nobody gone turn me around," she told the rattle of a lizard through dry leaves. And when she lay down on moss for her rest, she whispered for the spiders and copperheads to come on, make her their bed.

In Touch with God

IN TOUCH WITH GOD

Her first memory pulled her back to the rise and fall of her mama's breast and the slow steady swing of sacred harp singing.

"Hold my baby whiles I shout," her mama said. The hands that received her she couldn't recollect, but she remembered her mama's arms and hands widening away from her and then closing in on the spirit.

Her mama died before Roxie was five. Her daddy and her brothers raised her. She was the baby and some said spoiled.

By then she had heard enough of sin to know hers could bank the fires of hell, but she couldn't join her daddy's Hardshells until she reached thirteen and accountability.

She tallied up the dead babies on Copperhead and asked her daddy if they were playing dodgeball around the throne of God.

"Not hardly," he said.

She mourned for them.

He said, "What is to be will be."

She inspected the antlers of a lily, fingered the pup's chin and ran into the house to face the mantel clock and said, "The Lord God a Hosts knowed I'd do that at 8:31 on this Sabbath morn."

"Even the hairs on yore head is numbered," her daddy said.

In bed at night, she tried to count the hairs. She thought of all the full heads on Copperhead and God the Father up there keeping tally.

Such thoughts gave her the trembles. She blocked them out with the way a baby grinned when its navel was tickled, the way the thighs of Hirem Tiller played push behind a plow.

When she was twelve and a full woman, she shortcut her daddy's religion. On her way home from the store and post office, she stopped by the roadside to listen to the new Methodists sound out their brush arbor. The singing drew her bare feet to them, and when it started climbing Jacob's ladder she ran for the prayer log. The preacher sprinkled her on the spot from a tub of creek water he kept for the purpose.

That summer she learned to shout and faint. To run dancing up and down the aisle of the arbor. To clap hands in and out and to laugh deep from her bosom.

Her daddy tried to keep her from the day meetings. All night trips were denied. She sang to the top of her lungs, "I want to be a Methodist an' eat the Methodist pie. I want to be a Methodist, a Methodist till I die."

She got on his nerves and he let her go gallivanting.

The Methodist preacher saved or revived everybody who wasn't Hardshell or No-Heller. Then he got in his wagon to go sprinkle salvation on Tennessee.

The arbor wilted. Fell. Rotted. There was no church on Copperhead. The new Christians met at night in each others' homes to sing and preach and shout and faint. Roxie couldn't go.

When she finished her schooling at thirteen, her travel was restricted to a weekly trip to the store and post office. Funeral or a day wake, now and then.

At home she sang Methodist songs to hollyhocks, to the pup, to bean rows. But something was missing. Her mind slowly nudged out salvation and brought in the way honeysuckle smelled in moonlight, the way the hairs rose on Hirem's wrist when he waved goodbye for Ohio. She knew she had backslid when she couldn't remember the words to a single shouting song.

She was resaved at sixteen. Reverend Spivey, a free-willy Baptist, came to Copperhead to preach Ab Duty's funeral. He waved the parted Bible right at her and screamed that sprinkling was not enough, that to be saved she had to go under in the watery grave.

"If ye ain't been wet head to toe, Jesus'll spit ye out like a wad a corruption," he warned.

She feared water more than fire, but she let his hands cup her mouth and direct her head to the sandy bottom of the Stallard Hole.

He baptized eleven in one wading. He said he'd never seen a place so dried up in sin. He built a jack-leg church house and stayed for the summer.

One hot August night he licked his lips in Galatians and smiled at her. The next day they eloped to the county seat.

She thought her daddy would flail her, but he shook his head and said, "You've made ye bed."

She slept in it all through east Kentucky.

It didn't take her long to learn that Reverend Spivey had other beds to lie in. And when he remembered to sleep with her, he did night things she couldn't whisper to a living soul.

She caught a coal truck back to Copperhead but not to her daddy's beds. She took a job as housekeeper without pay for Ole Man Penley. He had been addled in a fall from his barnloft and he nightwalked. But he had a battery RCA, one of the first on Copperhead, and she got to hear God's word from afar. She would rush to hoe the garden, feed the stock, milk the cow and get back to front the radio.

She could dial God all the way to XERF Mexico. She found early morning monks in WCKY, Cincinnati, singing in unknown tongues. Reverend Buckhorn Bruce told her to lay a hand on the radio and be healed. She tried it. She got a tiny tremor.

Mixed up with God was *Everything Goes, Betty Crocker, Captain Midnight,* Portia who faced life. And wars and rumors of wars.

When somebody at the store said her ears were eavesdropping on hell, she hummed a song the radio gave her—"Get in Touch with God, Turn ye Radio On."

Sunday was all God, except for wars. Ole Man Penley's front room and porch were sprawled to overflow. She tried to cook and turn the radio's three knobs to Catholics speaking normal and in tongues. To all manner of Baptists, free willy and determined, shouting and calm. A Methodist from Texas who said he and his Jesus could stand on their heads. Pentacostals who danced to guitars and tambourines and, like the Catholics, spoke both ways.

Every Sunday night when she went to bed she tried to sort out what she'd been given. Love was good, but not with lipstick. If she had Jesus, she would climb trees, move mountains. Jesus was an A-1 businessman.

Sulphur. Prayer cloths. Parched tongues. Water from Jordan. Sand from Galilee. Rocks and mountains. Autographed pictures of Jesus Christ. Freewill offerings. Thieves in the night.

At day she looked long at the lips of roses, at pollen on the tassels of the corn. They helped to straighten out her nerves.

A Model-T load of Seventh-Day Adventists passed through in 1945 and said theirs was the church without controversy. For two dollars and dinner they wrote her name and Ole Man Penley's in the book of life.

Their message was simple. All Copperhead would die and then wake up to burn and die again, all because they couldn't read a calendar. Roxie counted to seven under the feet of the Dionne Quintuplets. The Sabbath was surely Saturday. She vowed to remember it and keep it holy.

The carload said if she did, she could wait a spell in Heaven till God charred out the sin on Copperhead and then come back to take up quarters. She liked that part. She dreaded eternal separation from phlox and beans and baby's breath.

There was no baptism. The river had run dry.

The new brand didn't stick to Ole Man Penley. He cried to listen to the banjos on a Saturday when sin spread general on the radio. She turned the RCA on for him. She stayed in the kitchen and looked at the calendar and tried to pray through all the talk of tonic and the songs of poison love.

Those who came to listen to God on Sunday took time out to watch her fight limestone and crabgrass in her garden. She chopped so hard she threw her lead wrist out of joint.

The Adventists had promised to come back to give her a booster. They never did. They sent one postcard of sinners and horses and dogs and cows squirming in a pit of brimstone.

Roxie tired of testifying for Saturday at the post office and the store, of hoeing for Sunday in her garden. She backslid all winter. Stayed indoors and listened to ever what her fingers found.

She stopped all denominational requests on Sunday. She kept the dials on the Holiness who were the loudest. Their music made her toes tap, made Ole Man Penley smile. Baptists quoted that strings were sinful and crammed fingers in their ears and fled the porch.

As if in answer to her dials, Brother Bobby Lee Necessary arrived on Copperhead and started The First Holiness Church of God in Jesus Holy Name, With Signs Following. He truck-mined on the side.

Roxie took Ole Man Penley's elbow and guided him a mile to hear in person the nighttime guitar, tambourine and mandolin. When the first verse of a song passed her by a second time, she joined in:

I'm gettin' ready for to leave this world,
Gettin' ready for the gates of pearl.
Keepin' my record right,
Prayin' both day an' night,
I'm gettin' ready for to leave this world.

Brother Necessary preached that water was not enough. "Just empties the soul a sin. Cleans out ye insides. Baptism in the Holy

Ghost fills ye up again, praise God!" He patted his jeweled cowboy belt that made a ditch in his belly and jerked his head so hard it seemed to roll out of its socket.

Roxie wanted more than water. She was the first to answer the altar call.

Brother Necessary's people put warm hands on her. Pressed the furrows of her brow. Played with the cups of shoulder blades. Felt the neck veins that jerked.

"Roll right in to the Pearly Gates!" they yelled.

The Holy Ghost hit her. It ran through members of her body she had forgotten she had. In spurts up to her head. In fiery prongs down to her toenails. She rolled for Jesus on the splintery floor.

She talked in tongues books hadn't taught her. "Huck shim mi ni o, huck shim mi ni i."

She did all sorts of things she never would have done in the natural. She rose to drape her neck over the shoulders of rank strangers. She even kissed some.

The next night she guided Ole Man Penley up to the altar. He liked the handling and was resaved.

They gathered with two other converts at the river. It was Ole Man Penley's second baptism, her third, not counting the sprinkle. But this one gave them sanctification.

Ole Man Penley caught a chill.

Brother Necessary came to the house to lay on hands and cure it and to help Roxie out with what Christians did after they were fired full of the Holy Ghost.

No lipstick, rouge, powders, perfume. No finger polish, no toe. No shaved armpits, rubber bosoms. No shortsleeved dresses. No ruffles anywhere. No bobbed hair. No rings, pins, bracelets. No Lord's name in vain. No *True Stories.* No hands under bed covers. No jigs, liquor, homebrew. No tobacco. No playing cards. No motion-picture shows.

She asked him about the RCA.

"What do ye listen at?"

"*Farm Report. Funeral Home Time.* Religious songs." She left out a favorite she had found, Hank Williams, whose voice could still night birds.

"Anythang's got God in it," he said.

He shook one last shalt-not into his head. "Don't live with a man ye ain't married to."

Brother Necessary hauled her and Mr. Penley in his mining truck to the county seat for blood and a license. He married them in the truck cab.

Roxie was partly whole. She prayed three times a day and at bedtime. She tried to keep the dials on God. When they nudged up on Hank Williams' wooden Indian or his crawdad pie, she cheated for a verse or two and then moved them on to the holy land chorus and the songs of Zion.

In the winter Brother Necessary went to Florida to save sinners in the sand. God went dry on Copperhead. She backslid by spending egg money on a mail-order enlargement of Hank. Her conscience hurt. She ordered a set of ten glow-in-the-dark pillows that spelled out JESUS SAVES.

When the church door reopened in late spring, she got back in one night her winter's loss. But Brother Necessary now preached a blessing she didn't know. Anointment, it was called.

"I want everythang 'at's comin' to me," she said.

"Ye'll have to go to West Virginia to find it," he said.

"What 'xactly is it?"

"Ye shall take up serpents," he whispered.

Roxie tossed and turned for a week of nights. She asked Mr. Penley what he thought. He smiled his sanctification to the radio.

She read and reread the verse in Mark: *They shall take up serpents.* It sounded strong. Woollyworms could fright her, but she figured they'd better go take their chances.

She wrapped a nose-rag around a razor blade and a little bottle of turpentine. She buried the wad in her apron pocket.

"We gone go git some anointment," she yelled into Mr. Penley's free ear.

Brother Necessary hauled them in his new car for gas and snacking money.

The Overcoming Pentacostal Holiness Church looked like the one back home, except nobody sat on the first three rows.

The music was better though. Three tambourines. Spoons. Two guitars. A banjo with the head of Jesus on its hide. A mandolin that could talk.

The singing started out slow. "Flowers for the Master's Bouquet." Then it gathered head to "Lord Build Me a Cabin in Gloryland." Higher still to "They Ain't No Grave Gone Hold My Body Down."

The saved gathered around the altar to pray and tremble fingers in the air to catch the Holy Ghost. Roxie propped Mr. Penley on a bench and joined them. The spirit came down so fast and hard she jerked the hairpins from her head.

There was no time for preaching. The brothers and a few sisters couldn't hold in the Holy Ghost. Reverend Lester Tinker unlocked the serpent box behind the pulpit and before Roxie could say praise-be-his-holy-name, he had copperheads and rattlers wriggling a necklace around his head. His eyes and mouth rounded from the load. His hands, scarred from bites he had lived through, rose toward heaven and then fell to wave the serpents on.

"Whoop!" Brother Necessary said and jumped right in.

"Let the Lord use ye," Brother Tinker screamed.

"Glory!" some sister yelled.

"If ye got the Holy Ghost, hit's gone come out," Brother Necessary said. His eyes glassed. His lips curled in a downward grin. He held a long diamondback with a blunt head. It curled toward Roxie.

"Shem-a-mi-ni-o. Sheckem. Sheckem," the worshippers said.

"Sheckem. Sheckem. Shem-a-mi-ni-o."

Roxie's fingers were playing in a pond of fish. The quiver moved on to her hands, cold, upwards to belly and breasts, down to thighs and legs. Her hands felt frostbit.

Jesus pushed her into the circle with the rest of them. She held her hands out to Brother Necessary.

He gave her the diamondback. She clutched it by its long tail and swung it around and around.

She heard singing far off.

"Hit's so low ye can't git under it."

She danced turkey-trot up the aisle.

"Hit's so wide ye can't git around it."

Children in the back rows ran outside.

"Hit's so high ye can't git over it."

She aimed the serpent toward Mr. Penley. He fainted out cold.

"Ye gotta come in by the door."

She cooed to the diamondback. Her head jerked toward it and then away. Her lips came close to the scales on its head.

"Gotta come in by the door."

Her feet grew warm. Then heat pronged up her legs to belly, breasts. Sweat trickled to every valley she had.

"By the door."

Before the spirit could get out of her fingers, she threw the diamondback to Brother Necessary who now had a free hand. He caught it and went into a whirl.

Roxie jerked her body quiet. She clutched the nose-rag in her apron pocket. She went to check on Mr. Penley.

He was still out. She fanned him with her aprontail.

"Home," he whispered.

They stayed a full week. They slept and boarded in the houses of the congregation. Roxie hoed in their gardens by day. At night, she handled serpents, sometimes the diamondbacks, sometimes scrub copperheads. She never put her hand into the box. She let the brothers do that. But when they had them free and wriggling, Roxie was one of the first to go grab. Mr. Penley declined.

On the sixth night, they built a fire in the potbellied stove. They took up hot coals in their hands.

The spirit worked the other way. Heat came to Roxie's fingers and she juggled the coals until the spirit began to leave her in a cold sweat. She didn't get so much as a blister.

The seventh night was for strychnine. Roxie read Mark again. *If they drink anything deadly, it will not hurt them*. It didn't sound as strong as the serpent verse. She drank seven dippers full of water before church. She and Mr. Penley sat in the back row.

But nobody opened the fruit jar on the altar. While Brother Tinker was singing "Satan's Pretty Pictures" to the big diamondback, it bit him on the neck.

They all gathered at his house to put on hands and hot cloths, but his head swole double and he died before tomorrow's sun could ever shine.

The brothers and the sisters gave the reasons.

"Could be a disbeliever in the crowd."

Roxie saw again her husband faint and the children run outside.

"Could be somebody thought the teeth was pulled."

The notion had crossed her mind.

"Or that they's froze."

Roxie fisted the wad in her apron pocket.

"Somebody might have had a little grudge."

Roxie shivered.

At the funeral she didn't handle a single snake. She and Mr. Penley stayed outside the graveyard gate. When the spirit was leaving those inside, they threw a diamondback and two copperheads into the coffin with Brother Tinker. The snakes tried to slither out. Brother Necessary slammed the coffin lid on the rattled tail of the diamondback. It wiggled as they lowered Brother Tinker into the ground.

"Home," Roxie said to Brother Necessary.

She didn't speak one word more in fifty miles of car riding.

Her backslide was the hardest that ever hit her. She turned the radio on and heard snakes hiss. In the garden cucumber vines struck at her.

She started to sing "Ain't No Grave Gone Hold My Body Down." She saw the diamondback rise out of the ground.

Her mind would have gone on her if Mr. Penley hadn't caught a cold and died.

She humped courage into her back and made his arrangements.

Her daddy's Hardshells came without asking to preach over him. He had been Hardshell in the original.

Brother Necessary's feelings were hurt. He chucked her. She was again memberless.

She traded the old house which was sagging for an abandoned one-room store out on the hardtop road. It had a concrete floor and the new electricity. And a rich garden. She swapped the battery radio in on an electric cathedral-front Philco and settled down to the tears Hank gave her when he sang "Loveless Mansion on the Hill," to smiles when he asked, "Hey, Good-Lookin', what ye got cookin'?" In between, she caught snatches of *Life Can Be Beautiful, Gangbusters, Baby Snooks, Young Widder Brown,* and new wars.

Alone at night, she bickered with the Great Guildersleeve. She got up enough nerve to tell Gabriel Heater he didn't know it all. But she never denied Hank Williams a stretch of his throat, a single rise of his Adam's apple.

One day she had an earache sweet oil wouldn't cure. She remembered Buckhore Bruce who had told her to put a hand on the radio. She did. Palm down on Hank and the last whippoorwill. She felt a tingle run all the way to her eardrums. She took her hand away. The pain was gone.

She tried it out on every crick and ache that crossed her body. It worked every time.

She drew a sign: GET IN TOUCH WITH GOD MIRACLE TEMPLE. Then, in littler letters underneath: Cures. She nailed it above her door.

At first the walkers up and down the road pointed and snickered at the sign. But those who had served time in the State Mental Asylum came inside.

Each day on her way to the post office and store, Omie Tiller stopped for a hand laying. She wanted Oral Roberts, but Roxie couldn't tell Tulsa when to broadcast. Omie settled on *Barrel of Fun*. She went away talking up Roxie's radio. She said it was like what the doctors gave her but not as hard.

Aunt Bethel Nuckols came for neuralgia. Went away whole.

Sister May June Hess for the dance of St. Vitus. Partly cured.

Omer Briscoe for piles. Helped.

Roxie didn't ask for a dime. She knew that if a healer grabbed for money, the gift would go. But she placed her sugar bowl by the radio. Some miners spared a dime or two.

The talkers at the post office and the store disbelieved in the radio. Some said it had a short. "Spatic 'lectricity," others claimed. Nat and Alafair said it wasn't grounded. When she heard, Roxie flapped the short sleeves of her new crepe dress and hummed "Get in Touch with God, Turn Ye Radio On."

The miracles grew. A man with a big Kodak came to snap her holding Hank's picture and palming the radio.

Her fame spread through three counties.

Her garden and flower beds suffered.

All denominations said the devil was in the radio, for Roxie let everything play, from *Milkman's Matinee* to "Say Can You See." She couldn't tell any difference between Thursday and Sunday, and the *Farm Report* did just as well as *Gospel Fires*.

If anything was strongest, it was Hank. "I'll Never Get Out of this World Alive" shrunk cancers. "Howlin' at the Moon" dried up female trouble.

A roving evangelist in a four-door car came all the way from Bluefield for a head cold. He tried to talk her into taking her Cathedral-front Philco on the road with him.

And she would have if Hank had not died on New Year's Day, 1953.

She took down her sign.

Closed the door of her Temple.

Hid her sugar bowl.

She pined and wasted away.

She died in what they said was her sleep.

The Sheriff broke in to find her propped and pillowed in her bed and only static playing on the Philco.

Everybody said she was rich, but the sheriff found no evidence.

There was no funeral service. She was memberless.

The County had to bear expenses.

Robbers broke into her house to rip open the mattress and the pillows that spelled. They took the radio, but only to Roxie's garden where Omie Tiller found it the next day. She swore it was fiddling to the winter crop of turnips.

Omie was so unnerved she had to be hauled back to the asylum.

Some schoolboys started to dig up Roxie's fallow flowerbeds for treasure. They said they heard Hank Williams sing out loud and clear. They ran over each other's feet to get away.

Most disbelieved. They said it was just the wind playing fiddle on the wires of the old electricity, the new telephones.

But to this day the strip-mine trucks pick up speed when they pass the hull of Roxie's Temple, and what few walkers are left cross to the far side of the road and, just to be safe with God, poke fingers in their ears and run on by.

The Garden

THE GARDEN

As a child, Tildy never played house. She played garden. In the sand by the creek while her mama washed, she set out Fool's Parsley and called it carrots. Ragweeds, young, were tomatoes, young. Wild mustard and onions came close to the real, and the early shoots of Lady Slipper could pass till wilting time for sweet potato slips. And Indian cabbage looked a lot like what her mama set out in even rows. Bush vetch, beans. Buck vines, beans. Bindweed, beans. Anything, greens. And burdock squash and pie-plant, too. Timothy, corn. Willow leaves, corn. Yellow flags, corn.

She watered them from the creek and when washday came again on Monday, she pulled out the dead and replanted.

In the real garden she followed her mama and the phases of the moon through the fresh-plowed furrows that with the help of hoes became rows, balks, rows, balks for an acre or more.

"Plant enough for the rabbits, for the birds," her mama said.

When Tildy was ten, her mama died because she would not let the doctor from afar saw off her leg.

Tildy proved to her daddy and her brothers and her sisters that the steps she had followed were faithful in their kind. And she saw that Willie, who had her mama's hands, knew how to lay off perfect rows, first with a string, then with just his eyes; how to build the different hills; how to sow the many beds.

As a married woman of fourteen, she planted her only tardy

garden. Hers was a July wedding, 1909. Too late for tomatoes, too late for beets. And Travis had only one new ground cleared at the foot of Wild Cherry Mountain. It was already planted in burley backer and almost ready to lay by.

While Travis felled virgin chestnut and pine for the new sawmills, she hoed the backer. Between each hill she planted a fall runner bean one-inch deep.

The beans came in in August, enough for a mess every day for a month and for wreaths of leatherbritches to circle two walls of the one-room cabin.

The backer grew tall enough to support its viney burden; but come cutting time, the leaves had limbered to the pull of the pods. On lugs upward through bright red and tips, the fingers of the beans had left their green. The crop was lost, except for home smoke, home chew.

Travis was mad until he looked at the pretty way her lashes butterflied when she tried to light a clay pipe. That winter he cleared more land up Wild Cherry and gave her the backer patch for a garden.

In late February, she dug in snow to bury the full heads of onions and waited for their prongs of green to make corn pone seem like new. She built and burnt and sowed a lettuce bed and dared a freeze to nip the early green. And March was for cabbage, mid-March peas, taters. Then carrots, beets. April was pepper and tomatoes and crooknecks and beans.

May 1 was special. She rose before dawn could dry the dew. She was careful not to hem or hum a word. She slipped to the garden to push into earth the white-sliver seeds of cucumber. Babies came that way.

By July 4, when the first tomato turned red, she knew she was in the family way, though her fingers couldn't find the swell.

It was stillborn. Travis pieced together a little box of pine and they buried it in the corner of the garden.

A false pregnancy followed, but the third May was a charm. The baby came in February, 1913, before the garden took prior claim.

Kentucky. Named, Travis thought, after the neighbor state he talked about, but really after the Wonder Beans that could climb as high as a pole could stake them. The baby got her father's face and his pout, which looked better on him. But she got Tildy's grip. The way she grasped a finger told Tildy she could someday hack a fast hoe through limestone to find the roots of crabgrass. Tildy built a cradle swing between two saplings near the garden gate so she could hoe while the baby learned to teeth on sweet turnips.

February 8, 1915, Missouri, after another Wonder Bean. The greenness did not take. Missouri had pallor from birth. More like icicle radish, without the fire. Tildy couldn't keep her in the cradle swing. Her skin couldn't take the sun. She was a good baby at night, but she caterwauled at day and made Tildy's hoeing harder. Tildy rolled her rosin balls, boiled sassafras, sumac, catnip; but they never brought a blush.

March 10, 1917, King, after her new-found beans that made the others runts — Kings of the Garden that would take over the world if their vines weren't trained to crawl up the outside walls of the corncrib, dairy, woodshed. King might have been considered a woodscolt if his lashes hadn't longed. He was prettier than Tildy had ever hoped to be, but he got her lashes that could bat once and find a hen's nest hidden from god. "Tildy her eyes," everybody said.

April 12, 1920, Simpson, after the black seed of lettuce. His curls found the jet of Travis' head before they saw daylight. "A heart breaker," everybody said, as their fingers fondled ringlets. The way he smiled to a tater or a crook-neck told Tildy he wouldn't break anything except the point of a bull-tongue now and then.

Tildy gave her womb a rest. And by the time Simpson was two, she had her first real Brag Garden. The cabin had squared outward into four rooms to take the yard and its bank of beehives.

The yard and beehives took part of the garden which marched again against Travis' backer and his corn. New outbuildings had to grow left in rocky soil. Smokehouse, chicken house, pigpen, barn. When Travis had cut most of the timber for up North, he rested his ax for saplings to grow and turned to shifting plots for Tildy's garden, her berry patches, and for enough pasture for three cows.

By then the early onion patch and the beds for pepper and tomato plants were as big as her first married garden. Kentucky walked and King tottered in the rows with Tildy while Missouri stayed inside out of the sun to churn butter and hush Simpson if he cried. Her bare feet could not be trusted in the rows. They bruised the tentacles of cucumbers. Bean pods hid from her fingers, for she would pull the whole vine to get one bean.

Tildy taught the hands of Kentucky and the eyes of King to measure the time by rows and the changes of the moon in the *Grier's Almanac*. Early March, when the sign was in the head or feet and the moon twixt new and full—cabbage, mustard, kale, and snow peas. As soon as the moon darkened, spring turnips, taters, beets, carrots, radishes. If Taurus refused to hoove his way into the dark, preferably in the Ides of March, the seeds and tater cuttings went in anyhow; for Tildy would not keep her favorites, beans, waiting beyond April 1, if the sign was in the arms. These were Early Wonders and with them come Sugar and Gold, the early corn. Tendergreen. And pepper slips looking shocked at all the brown around them.

April 7, Tildy's birthday, was for tomatoes. Earlinas, first, because they never let her down on the Fourth of July when she had to have a ripe one in order to say the mid-garden of the year was good. Their little globes were shamed by the later Big Boys. They were even smaller than the Yellow Pear, the Red, but they could and did lord it over the tommytoes that came up volunteer to give whichever was the baby something to play with.

Sweet taters came as soon as frost was unsuspected and darkness again claimed the moon. If the curling of the pea vines told her frost and the moon rolled ready at the same time, she elected the moon; for the slips, the whole garden, could be covered if need be.

Out came bedspreads, quilts, dresses, overalls, even dishrags to hide anything that resembled green. Her only fights with Travis were caused by her clothing of the garden, which by then was an acre. She volunteered him, Kentucky, and King—even Missouri held the lantern—to work into the night to give all except featherbeds and underwear to the rows and hills of promise.

Travis balked at each harvest of the house to sleep the garden. "Woman, we don't need the County planted."

The children agreed that first time.

"Plant enough for the rabbits," she said. "Enough for the birds."

"Hell fire an' damnation," he said.

She threw a clod at him and drove him from the garden. When he tried to make up by unlatching the gate, her eyes took aim with a rock.

If the sun the next day rose to kiss not frost, but dew, he smiled and she gave her eyes the stare that could turn flesh into salt. He would pout till late April—time to plant cushaw, pumpkin, summer squash.

Mid-May marked the end of the early garden, the top thirty feet set aside for melons. Muskmelon on the right; water on the left. The hills of the watermelons took more space than they deserved, for they never looked like the proud circles and the stripes the seed packets promised. The muskmelons grew one third their pictures, but they at least ripened. The watermelons never got bigger than dwarf cabbage. She blamed her one failure on the loam.

"Too rich," she said. " 'Ey's too much loam. Wisht somebody'd go to the river an' fetch me some proper sand."

Travis grunted. The river was miles away. Nobody ever went

there except to watch a baptizing or a flood.

For a month the garden was hoeing and gathering, weeding and dusting with wood ashes and coffee grounds. Then, as the garden stuff came in, new seeds were planted. Rows of peas, gathered and canned, became late corn — Country Gentleman White — and halfrunner beans. In August, when weeds prided, mattocks uprooted the mightiest to make way for late lettuce, turnips, hanovers.

Even in the first snows, green could be seen in Tildy's garden. Parsnips ripened in the cold. Celery crisped. And underneath the earth in rounded graves were taters, apples, cabbages, which could be brought to the table with a hoe and patient fingers.

Her garden grew. Mr. Henderson, who started a Baptist Mission school in '25, gave her children reading and ciphering for taters and corn. He brought Tildy okra from East Virginia, tree cabbage from Caroline. The Tallies built a railroad through in '28 for the North to mine the deep coal in the far tip of the county, and they swapped her a new green squash for her white rounded scallop. She couldn't talk to them with her tongue and her hands were shy around strangers, but the happy men could read her eyes and the arms of her children. A woman looking for ballets swapped her krauters for "Little Brown Girl," Swiss chard for "Little Naomie Wise." A Quakerman from New York came to build a dynamo to give the Mission School daylight at night. He taught her wild fern fronds and the tender shoots of milkweed. She taught him speckled dick and dry-land fish. She already knew the dandelions, the dock, the two kinds of plantain and of cress, but she had never seen their pictures in a book.

Coal men came through in '29 and paid Travis 50¢ an acre for what was under the ground. They didn't seem to care for the green that was on top.

Tildy lost Kentucky (1930) and Missouri (1931). Kentucky fell in love with the first Model T that came to Copperhead. A drummer was in it. He took her off to War, West Virginia, where she wrote that she missed her mama's kraut. She planted a garden, but they had to move often to keep up with the new routes. Each Christmas, till her family grew large and took her time, Kentucky sent Tildy a seed catalog.

Missouri married a coal-cutter who took her off to Dismal Branch. King said that when Missouri left, she waved goodbye to her pet cedar in the back yard and its hair turned white overnight. She and hers ate out of the new company stores. It was against the law to raise a garden on company land, but Missouri would have failed had she been free. On Dismal she learned to use the new paint, which King and Simpson claimed looked good on her when they went to visit, but she peeled it off when she and her husband came to take garden stuff for her babies.

Tildy got back in the family way to make up for lost time.

May 4, 1932, Ruby, for the red-leaf lettuce. She had the hands of Tildy's mama, hands that, alive, had learned to play without lessons an organ mullled from Roanoke. Slender and pretty as the lace they wove out of pea vines. Sure and steady to catch the prongs of tomatoes to tie and teach them upward. They fooled their delicate tendons to milk faster than Tildy's could, and hers were broad and patterned for a grip. Ruby's could cross-stitch, embroider. Tildy always said Ruby's hands could hatch eggs. Travis said they could grub hickory. They did both without show, for Ruby could be shied by a catbird's call.

September 20, 1934, Hubbard, for the winter squash. He got hands, too, Travis' that liked to feel the grain of a grindstone. But Hubbard's hands were wasteful in planting. For a hill that called for three grains of corn, two beans, he would drop five of each. If he was told to thin a beet row, he would bald it and make replanting necessary. He would pull the flowrets from Little Marvel Peas and pretend pennies. He saved tin cans and played store in the corncrib. But if Tildy promised a week's egg money for a harrowing, Hubbard grew new knots on his arms.

That same year, the railroad took back its train. It left the tracks for children to balance bare feet on. The dynamo and the Baptists left the school to go back up North, but Tildy kept what they had swapped her. She shared the seed with quilters who, in winter, walked from house to house to stitch Friendships. And she shared with those who came back from Ohio, where money had grown on trees. They told her about the Hoover times that never came to Tildy's garden. She gave them fresh and dried and canned vegetables. They forgot to return the cans.

Rationing came. Tildy planted sugar cane and learned how to can with sorghum. Coffee was scarce. Tildy returned to Mountain Tea and to the hulls of acorns parched.

Store merchants learned that Chinamen overseas chewed ginseng for a goodly price. They subtracted and saw green. King's eyes could catch one bee working a pond a horse hoof made and follow its wings to blackgums in the sky. They turned groundward to find the little red berries that spelled money. He quit the fields to find enough ginseng to transport him to the Mississippi River, where he washed his feet, and then on to the West and later to the Army and the World. He sent back a postcard now and then.

June 12, 1936, Cherry Belle, the radish. She liked the garden for its patterns, when the rows could be kept clean of weeds and volunteers did not crowd the balks. She liked to watch the short plants take their growth in front of the larger; the larger stand upright before the sugar corn that took the last, except for the melons that never mattered anyhow. In late summer, when the weeds had their say, Belle lost interest and turned to making neat the house, which Tildy never thought needed fussing. Belle would iron dishrags to get to listen to the batteries of the Philco Travis bought to hear the world.

November 30, 1938, Tildy's last baby. Kale. She had told herself she was too old, and the change did hit her as soon as he was born. He liked the green that could be picked wild—poke, sourgrass, plantain, ground cherries when they ripened. He didn't take to tame plants that stood when and where the seed packets told them to. But he was partial to taters with toes; to twin tomatoes; to carrots or turnips misshapened by rocks that crowded the roots and kept them home from fairs; albino cucumbers; squash speckled with the eyes of gourds; and sports. When an arm of a tomato or cucumber lightened it was not kin to that which held it, he cut the sport off and rooted it. He could make them grow big, but they never bore.

A great freeze came in '40 to take the beehives and Tildy's sparegrass, which had served first as food, then as decoration for the year. The chill reached even the deep roots of celery, of horseradish which had needed no care. She couldn't replace them, but the pie plant proved strong and the Jerusalem artichokes hid from the ice.

The Earlinas didn't ripen by the Fourth. Tildy fried some small green ones just to say she hadn't failed. The year's garden was not a Brag one. Spring and the moon were too late.

King wrote that the world was wider than he thought. Ships and airplanes, wars upon wars.

The next letter was from the Government and it was edged in black.

The skies had rained fire on Pearl Harbor. King was dead.

Simpson left his plow mid-row in the field, and before the body could come home with instructions not to open, he signed up with the Army for revenge.

King's body was planted in the corner of the garden, beside Tildy's first, the stillborn.

Travis stayed in the barn two days and talked to himself and played with fertilize.

From the insurance came a marble headstone, almost as long as the grave itself. With the rest Travis bought polled Herefords and a red wagon for Hubbard to collect and haul scrap metal in.

Tildy sang "Put My Little Shoes Away" to the rows in her garden. When her nerves would not let her sleep, she walked up and down the holler and sang "Will The Circle Be Unbroken?"

Truman brought Simpson home alive, with ribbons and badges. He tried to relearn the bow of the back that plow handles had taught him, but his eyes gazed far away. At night he talked in his sleep about bombs and shrapnel. And he would grab his bed-buddy Kale and squeeze him so hard he would cry. Simpson married a girl from Drill and moved there to augur coal in the Red Jacket Mines, where the new money was. He didn't come back home very often; for, when he had resting time, he drank Four Roses and swore by John L. Lewis' eyes. He died in a mine explosion in '49. His wife gave Tildy back the body for the family plot.

After the funeral, Kentucky took Ruby to Akron, her newest home. Ruby got a job in a munitions plant. Her hands found faulty bullets in an assembly line. She married a man as shy as herself. They didn't have any children. They collected license plates.

Locusts swarmed in '50.

A flood in '51.

The juice in '52. In Hubbard's first truck, a Ford car sawed in half with a bed added, Travis hauled home a refrigerator, a Maytag, and a deep freeze. Tildy preferred cans to the deep freeze, but Belle liked to pack vegetables in the little plastic bags.

Belle and Hubbard and Kale kept the lights on half the night to eavesdrop on New York and Chicago in a new electric radio. Tildy couldn't get her rest when night was day. She hid the light bulbs under some setting hens.

Hubbard and Belle said to her face that she was stingy and stubborn.

Tildy cut a switch for them. They outran her.

Hubbard bought a new truck on time and turned it into a money maker. He drove two shifts of miners to and from their work.

Cherry Belle caught his truck to Grundy, free, then a bus to Dayton, where she studied hair. She lived with Kentucky at first, but she and hers moved on to Arizona, and Belle stayed with Ruby, who had turned curious. Wore gloves night and day. Talked foolishness, Belle's letters said. As soon as Belle got her permit to make cold waves and hot sets, she left for Denver. In two years, she wrote back she could roll in greenback if she had a notion to. She sent Tildy a pressure cooker to can the years in, but Bethel Nuckols had lost her hair to one in an explosion. Tildy wouldn't use the little top that hissed.

Kale finished high school in '56. He wanted to go to college. Travis wouldn't fan his billfold. Hubbard said he could get him on at the mines.

Kale saw the crops laid by and then he thumbed to California. He sent Tildy packets of seeds she had never seen: Lovage, Basil, Dill. His last letter, from Canada, said he would like to be home plowing but he couldn't come.

The Lovage didn't last, but the Sweet Basil held its purpose for a time and the Dill spread its lace to the sun. Became volunteer.

Travis bought a tractor. Hubbard taught him to drive it up and down the holler. The land was too steep for its tires. Travis turned the wheel and talked to himself and played level farm.

He let Hubbard sell off the Herefords to invest in a trailer park near Grundy.

Hubbard tried to make more money when Travis died. He sued the tractor for the accident. Faulty brakes, he said, sent Travis over a hill and to a mangled death in the tractor's path. Hubbard didn't collect.

Kentucky, Missouri and Belle flew home for the funeral. Ruby's nerves, by telegram, could not take the travel. Kale could not be found.

Travis had deeded Hubbard the house and all the land. Kentucky and Belle fought with him in the kitchen.

Tildy didn't hear. She was gathering beans and corn for them to take back with them.

Hubbard said that the barn was too far for her walking. He sold the last cow in '62. He paid to have the house hooked up to the new phones that finally found Wild Cherry Mountain.

Tildy could answer the black crook but she couldn't dial. Her eyes, she said.

She also gave up the Almanac and the Bible.

The path to the pigpen slickened in winter to threaten her bones. Hubbard swapped the sow and her litter for a new electric stove. Tildy kept the old wood stove beside it in memory of its biscuits.

The pigpen became a wild garden of poke weed.

The crib fell. The woodshed. The smokehouse.

Hubbard couldn't take beans—simmered, fried, pickled, dried—seven days a week. He moved to Grundy to be close to his business and to eat T-bones.

He drew Government money to keep the land fallow. It saved him time and trips.

He came when he could to tell Tildy she'd better move up North.

The letters of Kentucky and Belle said come, but not to Hubbard.

Tildy stayed with the garden and her chickens and waited for Kale.

Belle sent a color TV to keep her company. She blinked at *The Price is Right.* At the President's men bouncing on the moon.

The weeds grew yearly downward in her garden—halved it, quartered.

The melons went. She could not afford the lingering space for their webbed feet.

Tree cabbage went. The green squash the Tallies gave.

Krauters. Chard.

The sugar corn became ten, five, then two drooping rows at the top of the garden.

But her eyes still saw the glory of turnips that purpled their importance, and her tomatoes blushed with the dew dribbled off them.

Kentucky said come. Do come.

Belle said come. Please come. You must come.

Tildy whispered for Kale.

Missouri asked could she bury her husband, dead of black lung, in the family plot. Tildy said yes, but Hubbard said no.

Missouri had to be satisfied with a graveyard of strangers.

Hubbard forgot to send someone to plow Tildy's garden patch.

Tildy dug it up with a mattock.

Ten rows tried to be an acre and only the hearty could take the crowding. The sweet pepper bells mixed pollen with the little yellow hot, and the fruit was bitter to the taste. Three kinds of squash came striped this half, spotted the other. She smiled at the crossbreeds and talked to them as if they were gimpy children that had to stay home from school or be laughed at.

She could no longer account for the motions of the moon.

Spring tried to be fall.

She planted all her okra seed, after soaking, in the snows of February. Not a plant peeped forth.

But beans were kind to her, even out of season. Mustard volunteered its spreading pattern. Tommytoes defied blight to ripen. Dill weed laced.

Hubbard came to show her a check with his name and many numbers. She was to move into a mobile home in back of his new brick house in Grundy. The land he had sold for stripping to The Nuclear Coal Company.

She left him standing on the sagging porch. She went to the garden to pull weeds for her five chickens.

The TV gave her the red lands of Jupiter.

She sat on the porch and waited for Kale and listened for the sound of Revelations to grind closer.

The Nuclear Coal Company moved into her vision.

Yellow land eaters large as houses. Bulldozers with blunt heads.

She watched them gut what had once been fields, pasture. The orchard.

Hubbard threatened the state asylum.

She waved her cane to circle the house and garden.

The richest seam was there.

The sheriff came with papers.

She told him she lived on Jupiter.

The telephone rang.

She didn't answer.

Hubbard came to plunder through the house and call out her name.

She hid in the cold dairy and counted beans.

Snow covered the red scars that surrounded her. The eaters lost their color, the dozers their blunt heads.

But when the rains came to bring the slides, she remembered the earth without form and void.

A doctor in a jeep told her she was a danger to herself. Slopping imaginary hogs. Calling lost cows at midnight. Crawling over boulders to find a chance sprig of dandelion.

She would not accept his ride.

Three sheriffs broke down her door. A chair turned backwards on the porch should have told them she wasn't home.

The bulldozers purred and waited for a sign.

A search party didn't find her.

On the third day, a whirlybird radioed a clump of color approximately 11,200′N of 36° 14′.

The County scaled the mud and rocks to get the body.

They had less trouble coming down.

Hubbard buried her and reburied the three others in perpetual care plots near Grundy. A tall cement Jesus opened hands for them.

The chickens went wild and perched like buzzards in the few standing trees.

Hubbard didn't come back to see why Tildy had crawled up the rock slides.

On the terraces the dozers had made, where some random loam mixed with the deep red soil and the bloom of coal, sprouted the tender spindles of bean vines, in crooked rows — an uncanny garden on the surface of some dreadful planet.

Afterword

What the Earth Gave Free in Appalachia

WHAT THE EARTH GAVE FREE IN APPALACHIA

Our Appalachian land was steep, rocky. Washouts often sent top-soil and crops to the rich river bottoms and on to the Big Sandy River and the world. A March wind could lift fires over mountains. The air itself could carry blight against tobacco plants. Underground slate could, and often did, crumble and kill.

Yet as children we could shudder off the post-Depression pain; for the same earth also gave—from tree and vine, from mulch quickened by April rains. Our calendar was not a checkerboard of dates decided by the bank and funeral home; it was a series of gatherings, of taking whatever the earth had to offer.

Strawberries came just before school let out for the summer. They flanked our every path. They carpeted our feet not yet callused against briars and bees.

As soon as the corn was planted, the tobacco set out, we had time for strawberries in larger patches. We could have found plenty near home, but we traveled up the holler and across the hills to Milton Keen's land on Harricane, where we lived during the worst of the Depression.

At the top of the mountain, we would sit on rail fences and listen to Milton deep in the holler. Perhaps he'd be stuttering plow commands to his mule or calling his ancient and deaf shepherd. Never, in all our trips, did Milton come to the upper half of his land where the best berries grew. His cattle, ten cows and a bull, claimed the wild pasture, but fenced from them were fallow garden plots around an abandoned house.

You had to choose your companions wisely for strawberry picking. The Halls, tenants on our land, would never do. They didn't have the patience to brush aside weeds and briars to get to the little berries. And Sissy, their only girl at home, would mistake fatigue for epilepsy, her mother's affliction, and we'd have to forget our buckets to carry her uphill and sometimes all the way home.

My sister Jo was an ideal companion. She might blink and wail in a cornfield, but she'd push through demons to get to something free. She could pick fast and she was wary, mute, knowing the shalt nots that accompanied most gardens.

There was no quiet when Minnie Ann Clifton came along with her. Minnie was so full of glee she frothed at the mouth—even when asleep. She might get half a lard-bucket full before she decided to bash it against the nearest head, and then spill what was left in paroxysms of laughter.

Her brother Garmon was my usual companion, especially after Jo learned to sing to *Hillbilly Star Time.* A born thief, Garmon was perfect for an hour, the time it took him to stretch his belly and to cover the bottom of his pail. Then he would start noticing snake roads in the grass, snake spit on every other weed, snake-doctors—dragonflies—thick as buzzards in drought. He'd run to the abandoned house to eat what was left in his bucket and to count ground squirrels, which, in his mind, fattened into wildcats.

I had no fear of the cats, though Garmon's father told of "painters" (panthers) that killed. I did fear the snakes. The large rockpiles below the best strawberry patch, where you could sit in one spot and pick half a gallon, were their playground—a fact attested to by the shed copperhead hides drying in the sun.

"Lordy-God-amighty-damn, what a rattler!" Garmon would scream and then go "Whoop! Whoop!" and dance on loose boards to sound doom.

At such times I despaired of him. I would have preferred picking the berries alone, but for snakebite and for the joy of finding a pod with eight berries, all in a dangle, and not a soul to show it to.

In the house, Garmon might last another hour, tearing off layers of fancy people on the old catalog wallpaper—time for me to fill both my peck buckets.

On the way up the mountain, Garmon rocked the cows and bull. With nothing to weight him down, he could skin a tree. I had to watch and pray. Though Milton Keen's bull looked like an overgrown yearling, he had butted Sidney Owens over a ten-slat gate.

At the top of the mountain, we rested. Grazed on sourgrass (sorrel) at our fingertips. Dug goober-peas with our hands and ate them. Maybe wild onions on a dare. Whatever the fare contrasted with the berries that stained our faces.

We popped leaves. Rolled rocks to see if we could hit the creek a half-mile below. Garmon might catch a dung-beetle (June bug to romantics), tie a string to one of its legs and whirl it around for a buzzing kite.

On our way down we peeped into birds' nests in low limbs, on stumps, on the ground itself, especially the silken purses of humming birds. And Garmon, unlike Estil Johnson, did not break the eggs. Estil would pull the heads off baby birds, so people would know he was around.

Garmon and I took our time. Headiness and gravity would have toppled us had we rushed. We checked last year's ground hog and rabbit holes to see if they were in use. New smaller ones I guessed to be the homes of crawdads, but Garmon saw them as the hatcheries for rattlers.

We stayed clear of cliffs and caves where Haskew Fletcher lived, when the asylum let him out on furloughs.

I stopped at Garmon's house: a barn, really, closed up slightly against the wind. His mother often gave us batter-bread with an icing of old butter.

Garmon would have plenty excuses for his empty bucket: "Fell an' spilt every last one." "Milton's bull got atter me, clumb a tree an' stayed up it."

When he and I traveled to the hard-top and the river, I always shared my store treats; but I guarded the berries, now covered with poplar leaves.

To enter your own yard with two pecks of wild strawberries was to be a hero briefly, for capping them came next. A tedious job, one of such subtraction that only a gallon of little knots would be left, reduced partly to juice by the heat, partly by the force of fingernails that pried the green from them.

In most families, any male over 11 did not have to cap strawberries. At Hattie's house everyone gathered under the apple tree in the front yard. A communal container was placed in the middle of the circle. Smaller lids and plates held individual mounds of pods and berries and we started the intricate work. Our mouths watered, but we did not dare eat this late in the process. The juice, forced where splinters or hangnails had been, burned as would iodine.

We never threw away the white ones. They gave a tartness to the preserves — the best use for strawberries, thick in its own pectate, sufficient reason to get out of bed in February.

The berries went straight from the yard to the cookstove, kept fired all day to catch summer. When the preserves had thickened, children got to spoon the kettle. Then the youngest, a niece or a neighbor's baby, licked it. We could not eat — waste — the actual preserves until winter, for the garden was already giving mustard, lettuce, onions, snow peas.

After each canning, we counted the proud quarts and pints lined up on the screened-in porch and then, for room, moved them to the dairy in back of the house or to boxes under the beds.

Raspberries came next, and seemingly overnight. Tiny green circles of grains would swell into burrs, blush into cranberry red, then into purple. With hands still dyed from strawberries, we turned to briars, called vines, closer to home. It was as if the raspberry needed human protection for its delicate mauve whip that signaled next year's fruit. Our garden was surrounded by them. A few even grew in the balks of corn, potatoes. To Hattie, killing a raspberry vine was to deny grace, for you could almost put your bucket under the vine and shake the rich berries down; that is, if you waited for them all to ripen at once. Pickers who knew the berries' value never did that. Birds forgot grubs to reel on the dark wine of raspberries. The gathering then had to be in spells about three days apart. Mama picked most of ours. They were her pets, close enough so she could check the cookstove for whatever was on it, protect the garden from chickens, the baby chicks from the hawks circling in the sky.

On our way from hoeing in the fields, we would sometimes fill a shirtail or dress-lap with raspberries to supplement their two grand purposes: dumplings for immediate feasts and jam for winter. The dumplings had a palm wad of berries and a few pinches of sugar inside flour-dough. The balls were boiled until the skins showed slight purple. Each midday in raspberry season the dumplings were served hot; each supper we had them leftover and cold, but just as delicious.

Dewberries came right at the end of the raspberries and the beginning of blackberries. Though no one took them seriously, they could bring a little joy to field work. They seemed to like the spaces between cleared land and forests: the fringe above and below the fields. They grew on ground-trailers, in grass and weeds. Feet, not hands, found them — a prick that would make you look down to see what wanted you: knobs smaller than blackberries and sweeter — musty, hinting of the dew that fell just after midnight. Plump and blackened, they left their brief sugar in the mouth and mind.

Some pickers mistook the dewberries for blackberries, their

cousins — so vulgar they could be used in war and flirt games. Thrown to dumb chickens as joke corn from Brobdingnag. We didn't have to go searching for blackberries; they came crawlng to us. Two or three rough briars one year would be twenty the next. And scythe and axe would have to be wielded against them, or give up part of the orchard, the pasture, even rockpiles.

Yet we skirted vines heavy with fruit to cross the hills again to Milton Keen's. We claimed that the ones there were bigger, juicier, but maybe we wanted to stand on a spur and look over at the holler where most of our memories lay. We could actually see the Johnsons at work. Hear the plowman curse or praise. See the hoers stretched out across a field. But the distance of a half-mile was as far as Jo and I would go. Our neighbor Maudie had died there of hunger. Our sister Eleanor, after only a few days of life. Daddy had been crippled. And we had despaired of any purpose beyond the front yard.

The Halls had also lived on Harricane. They went with us blackberrying — and, behind them, their scruffy fiests. Sissy ate whole patches within the rings of the bull's breathing, then fainted if someone hurt her feelings. Once the two oldest boys caught the bull by the tail and nose, twisted both, and sent him bellowing to Milton, who thought snakebite.

Their mouths and bellies purpled, the Halls might drop a few of the firmer berries into a pail for their nephew at home, their mother back from the mental asylum, their granddaddy, Uncle Zack, the oldest man on earth; but they were mostly waiting for the dogs to hole something.

At the first yap they rushed to the quarry, so often in the snakey rockpiles. There they helped the dogs dig through sandstone and limestone, sometimes for one skinny rabbit but often for a ground hog fat on greenery.

Jo and I filled our four buckets. We took the shade to rest. We might fan Sissy, flushed with the threat of faint. Actually she was suffering from precocious puberty—at eight. The little nubs showed it. We might hide our berries and walk down for the taking of a ground hog, the cutting of a stick, poking it into the hole until hair stuck to its point, moving more rock and dirt, keeping the dogs from tearing the animal to pieces when it was cornered and held. But the ruckus might bring Milton. He didn't want his rockpiles scattered, and we had already seen the hunt. We generally waited for them to lug the five-to-twenty-pound ground hog uphill.

We walked home in a line: hunters first, their faces stretched in glee; dogs next; then pickers; and Sissy, wiping her brow.

Jo and I shaded our berries at the Hall house and waited for the feast: ground hog boiled tender and then peppered and baked brown. It was served with biscuit pone, the only good sop-bread, but a weak napkin against the drip.

That the Halls had gone blackberrying was forgotten. But they had no money for cans and sugar. Poverty and mismanagement had made them true carpe-deists. Canning, preserving, drying, salting, holing things up—apples, cabbage, potatoes—in the ground. These required a tomorrow. After years of wasteful gloom—and glee—they could not suddenly become New Dealers.

Mama gave them stuff for the coming winter, but they opened the cans the same day, even if the contents could be had fresh from the garden. "God will provide," said the one-eyed father and the ancient granddaddy, neither of whom could read the Bible they loved to quote. What they meant was that in summer two wiry fiests would sniff out meat and, in the winter, Hattie Ball would see they didn't starve.

After the Halls moved away, we had the Duties as neighbors. Their father worked in the mines at night, on the farm by day. The mother and twelve children raised a garden that would set most farms to shame. And the Duties were adept at picking anything that sprang from the earth. At blackberrying they carried not only buckets to Milton's fields, but also tubs.

The Duties had a blue-tick hound and a mongrel. The boys would answer them once the tubs and buckets were filled. Yet the Duties didn't eat ground hog any more. "Stuff tastes right wild," they'd say. They preferred fried bologna, Kellogg's corn flakes left to soak overnight in milk, and the old-timey blackberries. One year their mother put up 365 cans for pan pies.

Only one other important berry remained: huckleberries, rare once the forests had been razed for sawmills and mining props. Huckleberries grew high in the mountains, and they ripened late in the summer when snakes were the meanest. We rarely saw rattlers, but we had been told they lived and loved under huckleberries. Even brave souls carried long hoes to pry into the low-lying bushes before hands would lunge for the tiny grains: blueberries condensed in size, quadrupled in flavor. On Harricane, the older children picked them each year.

In our new home, Jo and I had other employment in late summer: the "cash" crops of May Apple and lobelia. Other herbs — pennyroyal, yellowroot, bloodroot, poke, catnip — could be sold, but for next to nothing. May Apple roots brought 8-10¢ a pound; lobelia weeds, 15-25¢. Jo and I were experts at finding and harvesting both.

May Apple grew everywhere, but most profusely on Milton's land in patches of deep shade. Jo and I never told our friends we were going digging. We either slipped by their houses or walked all the way through woods. This business meant lunches at school, books, Christmas. We carried tow-sacks, half-handled hoes. At opposite sides of a bed of the sleek umbrellas, we'd start our digs and work inward until our sacks were filled with the roots. To inhale them long would make you dizzy, even sick; but to have a sackful bouncing on your back was to perfume the path around you.

Pulling lobelia, called low-billy, was even more secretive. Long before the wood's tiny blue flowers became seed, we would case out fields. We knew every new ground and corn patch that lay fallow from last year; there the weed grew best. Solitary shoots could be found almost anywhere, but seeking these out was not profitable.

We timed our raids according to the plants' maturity. Else it would weigh little. Most thieves also planned the time of day, when the land's owners might be less likely to know: just at dawn. Snakes didn't travel, we were told, but Jo and I had morning chores. Older rogues took advantage of the night. We had to grab when we would, in the heat of the day, on our way home from the store and post office. Open criminals, we'd hump our backs and ape-walk into Jim Hale's fields, the best, in the holler next to ours. He and his wife seemed too old to tally the worth of weeds, but their dogs knew we were around. We listened for changes in their barks as we pulled the peppery weed that caused itching and burning, especially when it mixed with sweat and rolled into the eyes. But we'd move a sea of ragweed in our frantic grazing. At the end of self-appointed swaths, we'd pile what that row had given us — always on the get-away side in case we had to outrun buckshot. We worked until the dogs got close and our breathing almost stopped from the momentary asthma the weed could cause. We hid for tomorrow what we could not carry in bales on our backs. At home we'd say we found a fortune on the riverbank, free territory for all.

With paring knives, to save as much weight as possible, we carved off the roots and spread the tall weeds on the tin roof of the coal-wood shed or the tarpaper roof of the corn-crib and dairy. May Apple roots were dried there, too. If rain blew up in the middle of the night, we butted darkness to save our crop. One long day of drying and the low-billy could be bundled and taken to Eb Fletcher's, Marthie Ratliff's, or Ive Compton's store. Perhaps we'd find a new batch, on the way home.

We knew which merchant was offering the best price; we knew

too which ones had light scales or docked us for dampness. We *could* strike back: nails or wire rammed up larger stems; a rock tied firmly in the middle of a bundle.

When electricity came to the main road in the late '40s, Jo and I would waste a nickel on ice cream. The rest went for things we needed at home: coffee, salt, sugar; mama would then give us cash. No merchant bought with money, except for ginseng, which grown men hunted.

"Clever," people said for Jo and me, the same word they used for our parents. If only they had known that we not only nabbed weeds but that once, with Minnie Ann and Garmon, we broke into an abandoned store and stole one shoe, a bottle of Kool-Aid before it became powder, and two hairbows spotted in mildew.

Our greed, or enterprise, was responsible for one great shame. Garmon's father told Jo and me that Eb Fletcher was buying creek rocks. "Just the white kind," he said. "None 'em sandstones. Two pennies a pound."

"Low-billy brangs a quarter," one of us said.

"But hit don't take many rocks to make a pound," he said.

Jo and I walked on tiptoe until we were out of his sight. And then we ran for the Russell Fork, a creek called River, which it was in floods. We wanted to get a jump on others who surely would rake the riverbed tomorrow.

Once in full sweat, Jo started having doubts, though I could understand how rich folks up North would want the beautiful rocks for decoration. We didn't know what May Apple and low-billy were for; maybe the white spots cured some disease.

But after building three large pyramids, hastily covered with ragweed, we walked to Eb Fletcher's to wait until the store cleared for me to ask him the going price of creek rocks.

Eb Fletcher generally treated children as equals, but he hitched up his pants and looked around for some silly cat to grin at. He could only bounce off us the high whine of his laughter.

Hoodwinked, beetfaced, we returned to sparse lobelia.

The story of the creek rocks spread. But Eb never gave our names. Just "two fool youngens" — stock for laughter into late August when school, chores and real harvests kept us in line.

Afternoon cow-hunting and Sundays we might use to gather what the woods now gave: paw-paws too rich for more than one glutting; haws; elderberries, bitter, but beautiful in their sprawl. Nuts: hickory, hazel, beech, butter, black, chinquapins. The hickory, beech, and chinquapins we ate then; the others we saved for winter and, maybe, fudge.

Two special treats came with the first frost: persimmons and fox and possum grapes. The persimmons were not those monstrous globes we now find once a year at the green-grocer's, but dark, wrinkled knots the size of tommytoes, salad tomatoes which grew volunteer. Their sweetness caused many a child to founder, mouths drawing inside out from the addictive alum. Fox and possum grapes were impossible, until the cold taught them sugar. The fox variety were then the runted cousins of "northern" grapes. The possum kind remained wild but delicious, even after two frosts. To spend a schoolless and golden October day in trees ribboned with fox and/or possum grapes was to guess a little of what birds know at birth.

On crisp weekend nights when still air hoarded scents, we might go hunting for possum. A trained dog was needed, not old Brownie who could tell when something was in the hen-house, but who was scatternosed in the woods.

Our brother Pasco, home from Berea College, decided to get rich as a hunter and trapper while he taught seven grades in a one-room school high on Fletcher's Ridge. Monday through Thursday nights he lived in a smokehouse with a battery radio. Friday to Sunday nights he lived with us, three steep and curvey miles down. The owners of the smokehouse were also the masters of Blackie, the best possum-coon dog around. On Pasco's Friday walks home, he dangled pork-skins before Blackie's nose and mouth. The dog followed.

We fed him double to make forget master and home, and, at night, we headed for spurs rich in grapes and persimmons. At Blackie's first growl, we turned him loose and we would sit and wait for either the high bark of something up a tree, or for the low bark of something holed. The latter we ignored, too much trouble at night. But we'd climb the highest trees and shake down possums for the dog to worry into submission. The following morning, we'd have possums to skin — their meat given to the dogs, their hides stretched onto slat boards.

The thickest furs could bring up to 50¢. They were used for collars on women's coats, in catalogs. Yet our hides hung moldering on the woodshed wall next to the rusty traps Pasco ordered from Sears. Someone a county away had caught a mink. Pasco believed that otters and muskrats would leave a full river for our tiny creek, especially if he rubbed Miracle Mink Oil on the steel. We caught only possums, their bladed heads a diagram of stupidity.

When Pasco went back to college, this time in Ohio, Garmon and I tried our hand at trapping down by the big pine where we'd seen strange tracks. Ten minutes away, we heard our first victim, a mangey stray dog who ate with our hogs. We had to work a nervous hour to release him, accomplished only when we threw our coats over his head and wrestled him still to loosen the metal jaws. We never set another trap. We had seen terror.

In deep winter, the land gave little: snow cream, perhaps; the black berries of sawbriars almost petrified from cold. Jerusalem artichokes, if we could dig them from the frozen ground. Rabbits for the brave. (They were said to carry a deadly disease.) Squirrel for those who had dogs trained to tree.

At least one Sunday we spent in the woods gathering special kindling for the fireplace and the cookstove. With hatchets or axes we knocked off the knots on rotting pine trees, or dug up parts of stumps. To inhale the rosin was to know the cleanliness of winter and to feel ahead to warmth, for the knots and stumps, split into small strips were as reliable as kerosene to start morning fires. The larger pieces we threw and rolled downhill; the knots we put into sacks to drag behind us.

We knew the first promise of spring at school when Mrs. Wampler brought long shoots of pussy willow for her many vases. And the janitor, more respected than the principal, tapped the sugar maples that lined the path between the grade and the high school. He never caught enough for syrup. He let us drink the sap from the pails. We smacked our lips on the taste of bark. Staggered in mock drunkeness.

Mid-March, we picked our first "sallet" on hillsides not already plowed. To dandelion and broad-leaf plantain, the two best, we added, for spice, a little white dock, wild radish, wild mustard, dry-land cress, sorrel. Speckled-dick and red dock for their color. For more sweetness: wild lettuce, lamb's quarters, pussley, shepherd's purse. And, for good measure, the leaves of violets. The greens were a bouquet, their juice a nectar for the passing of the cold.

Pokeweed we treated special. Its tender shoots we rolled in meal and flour and fried in pork drippings. The taste was that of exotic fish which we so craved.

Easter flowers had by now bloomed in every yard. Daffodils. And in the woods, redbud which we ate by the handsful. Hardly a square foot of wildness was without some show.

And the orchards gave their tamer glory: apple, pear, peach, plum — all broadcasting a perfume that could make a child lie down and listen to the bees instead of tracking the heavy hooves of cows.

The first fruit was sarvices, called such for the "services" at Easter. The tiny red cherries grew in thick woodlands. The taste was medicinal, though children rode the bushes to the ground for the tonic.

The bitterness could always be chased with the scraped inner-bark of birches. Its minty sweet sap took us back to winter. And the pulp which the hungry swallowed could bring gut ache more pronged than that caused by green apples.

Rhododendron and mountain laurel now fringed every hillside. To get the teacher's grace, children carried to school armloads of the sprays. They washed away rancid winter: toe-jam, underwear not changed for months, the stench of toilets.

The prize for perfume and beauty went to the wild honeysuckle, actually azalea, which unlike their tame cousins gave a hypnotic sweetness from every bearded trumpet. Most of the bushes, usually on weak soil around bluffs or spurs, bore salmon-colored blossoms, though the hue was never the same. Now and then we would find an albino-white. Once a decade, a pink. Once a lifetime, perhaps, a yellow. What prodigals we were to break the limbs of such miracles to take them home for show.

Honeysuckles could be combined with the best search of all—for dry-land fish, morel mushrooms, or markels, merkels, the small sponge cones that now rival truffles for the rich. In early April I would keep close watch on a dying apple tree in the far corner of our garden. That tree always had at least one morel, a flag for what might be. After any long night of rain I would hide my books in rhododendron and head for the north side of the few woods not disturbed by loggers. Under beeches that spread wide crowns and roots I might find some: small, dark, almost black on the outward reach of the sponge and whitish tan inside, where woodants loved to feed. Eyes had to be keen to detect the fragile nods in mulch packed down for decades.

But Marthie Ratliff's orchard was where I was ultimately headed. In summer the gnarled trees there bore a few tiny knots of wormy apples. Peaches and plums that never ripened before their skin took the jellied glue of insects and their eggs. But in spring these weak trees umbrellaed the cones of spores, as many as eight under a single trunk.

I carried my paper poke gingerly, resting now and then to breathe the gather: distilled dew; the breath of dolphins; the night sweat of Druids on a ramp.

All ordinary supper plans were forgotten. Without knowing it we were in Paris, brokers of great wealth.

We rinsed the mushrooms in a dishpan of cold water. Halved them with a careful knife. Drained them on chopsacks that doubled as dishtowels. Rolled them in cornmeal.

We fried them quickly in butter, preferably aged into flavor. We ate them with cornbread and milk, though old-timers said that sweetmilk with dry-land fish would cause certain death.

Jealousy, surely. Anyhow, we could not be bothered by mortality, not with morels as our fare and as prelude to months of reaching out and taking that which the earth offered in its kind and gentle roll.